Madolina's Daughter

Lisa Sita

Author website: lisasita.com

ISBN: 978-1-7344697-0-7 (paperback)
ISBN: 978-1-7344697-1-4 (eBook)

Library of Congress Control Number: 2020900928

This is a work of fiction. Historical events, real places, and references to real persons are used fictitiously.

Cover painting: Claude Monet. *Bordighera*, 1884. The Art Institute of Chicago.

*In memory of my parents,
with love and gratitude*

Chapter One

On a bright December morning in 1947, with the war behind us and an uncertain future in front, I left my home in San Vittorio in the fragrant, rustic mountains of Calabria. My brother Taddeo, big for his fifteen years, and my mother, whose occasional coughs I recognized as attempts to ward off crying, walked on either side of me to the main road that led down our mountain and to the train station at the seaside town of San Michele. A small crowd of friends and relatives followed, chattering amongst themselves in the cool sunshine, and behind them, carrying my suitcase, was Uncle Enzo, my mother's brother, who would accompany me on the train to Naples, to the port and the ship that would take me away. Once on board, I would be on my own on the long voyage west to America.

"You'll write to me as soon as you get there?" asked Taddeo. He was taller than I was, and as he looked down into my upturned face, his eyes were shiny and moist.

"Of course," I said. "And I'll write every day after

that. I promise."

He smiled. "I'll join you soon, Alba. As soon as I can, I'll come to New York and build skyscrapers. And I'll bring mama with me."

He was quiet after that as the dirt crunched beneath our feet. When we reached the road, the little group of well-wishers encircled me, and I was caught in a series of hugs and kisses and appeals to keep them all informed about life in America.

Then my mother approached me. Her embrace was a soft crush, loosening the slivers of glass barely held together in my chest until her touch sent the delicate weave crashing down within me. I held tight but refused to cry for fear of losing control, and she could not let go.

This small, modest woman who had borne me twenty-one years earlier was my reason for leaving—she and only she, a mother who was an anomaly in that ancient place of patriarchs. While other mothers waited for their sons to come of age before sending them hurtling across the ocean to a more prosperous life, mine found value in the untapped strength of daughters. When the women and men of the town warned her about the dangers of sending an unaccompanied girl out into the ferocious world, she deflected their concerns by reminding them of my intelligence and good sense. When they chastised her for her careless disregard of my endangered virginity, which I would surely lose in the wilds of New York, and for her indifference to how shameful it looked for a girl to travel unaccompanied, she discounted their words with a flick of her wrist and a tart response for them to mind their own business. She—Madolina, the midwife of San Vittorio—was sending her daughter to become a nurse in America, and she was sending me to my father, after all. That would quiet them for a while, until someone's imagination, enslaved to tradition, created new and ever more distasteful scenarios of what could go wrong with a girl set loose in a foreign, decadent country. She ignored them all.

I breathed softly into her hair. "I can stay," I said.

My words released her hold on me, and she gently backed away. "No, Alba." She sniffed. "You go."

I was not sure I could. I was not sure I could turn around and walk away from her, from Taddeo, and from all I knew of the world without crumbling into the dirt and grass at my feet. I felt no courage, no excitement, only a sense of duty, and I would have turned back to San Vittorio rejoicing if only she had said the word.

But she didn't. She took another step back to make room for Taddeo, his eyes now fully red from crying, to approach me with a goodbye kiss. He stood still at first, as if afraid to touch me, but when I reached out to hug him he grabbed a tight hold and only let go when my mother pried him loose from my arms.

So I left them there on the edge of our town and continued down the mountain with Uncle Enzo.

I spoke little on the train ride to Naples, giving my full attention to the changing scenes beyond the window and trying not to think too much about the future. Uncle Enzo tried his best to raise my spirits with jokes and small talk and family stories I had heard before. "Think of all the wonderful things you'll see and do in America," he repeated several times, and each time I smiled and nodded.

When he left me at the dock and the waiting passenger liner, I hugged him tightly and quickly boarded the ship with a gnawing hollowness in my stomach. "You be careful," he called after me as I left him. I did not turn around.

That evening, standing on the deck, I looked out at the lights of the city spread like a sparkling mantle thrown casually across the land. Its war-shattered beauty hurt me. There it lay, open and inviting, sitting at the edge of the bay from which my ship was slowly pulling away, heading towards the bottomless black waters of the Atlantic. I left only when the dinner bell rang to take my meal silently in the dining room. When I returned, the magical image of Naples had disappeared. All that was left was a giant sky of cold bright stars and the splashing of waves against the hull as I stood there, alone in a dark void.

In the days that followed, storms in the Atlantic sent walls of water crashing over the decks. Passengers sickened and lay moaning in their cabins. I was spared the nausea thanks to the bag of dried chamomile flowers my mother had insisted I take with me. Each time I sat down for a meal in the ship's dining room, I would request a cup of hot water and steep my own tea with the flowers. It was a common remedy for stomach ailments and always effective. Had it been possible, my mother would have sent me along with a live fig tree in addition to the chamomile. Many times in my childhood she had cut a twig from one of the fig trees in our yard, slit it to release the sap, and stirred the twig in a pot of boiling milk until the sap formed a custard on the milk's surface. Adding a little sugar sweetened the custard's stomach-soothing properties and made a nice treat. But here on this ship, without a fig tree in sight, I was grateful I had my mother's chamomile to drink.

Each day on board was the same for me, sitting on my bed watching the force of the water lashing against the portholes. For all its smallness, my cabin was comfortable, with its wood paneling and soft narrow bed, paid for with money my father had sent from America. There was little to keep me occupied, so I spent most of my time with my books, precious things I had ordered by mail all the way from Reggio Calabria. There were language books that helped me learn English, novels that conjured up places to which I could thankfully escape from the retching sounds the thin walls did little to conceal, and history books with glossy photos of European cities.

The books also distracted me from worrying about what lay ahead, of how I would get along in a strange place where the language was not my own and where I would be living with a father I barely knew. Since I was an infant, he had been going to America for years at a stretch, working there and sending money back to my mother, until he had crossed the ocean so many times he had become a stranger to us. Sometimes a vague recollection passed through my memory of a kind face with deep brown eyes. I remembered him more in sounds and sensations than in visual images: a soft-spoken voice, the scent of pine, a gentle laugh that always made me feel like it was summer. When I was five, he returned one September morning and stayed the whole time that my mother's belly swelled. I thought he would remain then, but a few years after Taddeo was born he was off again, and the envelopes with the New York postmark came regularly once again to the tiny post office in our town until his next brief visit. Then the war broke out, and all correspondence stopped. When it resumed, four months after the armistice, the funds he wired home to us were more generous, but the envelopes came less frequently, and the letters were short. On the day I left

San Vittorio, I had not seen him in twelve years.

One dim afternoon, a gray-eyed young man knocked on my cabin door. I had seen him often in the ship's dining room, always at the same table within a cluster of other young men, although the epidemic of seasickness kept many confined so that the group was always changing from day to day.

"Excuse me, I'm sorry to bother you," he said in an unfamiliar dialect. "My name is Vincenzo." When he realized I had trouble understanding him, he switched to standard Italian. It was the most useful way of communicating on the ship, where passengers came from various regions. "I noticed at breakfast this morning that you were reading, and I was hoping I might borrow a book from you. It's taking a very long time to cross this ocean, and I'm getting bored."

There was something in the tone of his voice, some sweetness like the scent of rotting apples heated by the midday sun, that caused me to pause. He did not look like someone who read the kinds of books I liked. He looked more like someone who preferred to spend his days in the local café with a packet of cigarettes and a deck of cards, but who was I to judge?

"I suppose I can lend you something," I said.

My books were piled in short, neat stacks on the bed. As I ran my fingers over the spines, searching for something suitable, Vincenzo remained standing in the doorway. I decided on a copy of an Italian translation of *The Three Musketeers* and handed it to him.

He glanced at the cover, flipped quickly through the pages, and smiled. "Thank you," he said, handing it back to me, "but this looks too long to finish before we arrive in New York."

A strange statement, I thought, coming from someone bored by a long trip.

Vincenzo's gaze moved around the tiny room and landed on a scalloped-edged photo that lay on the small dresser beside the door. "And who is this?" he asked, reaching from the doorway to pick up the photo.

I took it from him. He was getting far too familiar.

"I see," he said. "A sweetheart left behind?"

"My husband," I lied.

"A husband who sends his wife across the sea on her own?"

"That's none of your business."

"Forgive me," he said, "I was only concerned for your welfare."

"My welfare is not your concern. My father is meeting me in New York. Would you like a guide book? You don't have to read the whole thing, just pick out the parts that interest you." I handed him the *WPA Guide to New York City* my father had sent to me a few weeks before my departure. With the help of an Italian-English dictionary, I was able to learn the names and locations of the city's main attractions.

"This is written in English," he said.

"Then use a dictionary."

He shrugged, holding out his hands.

"You didn't bring a dictionary? How do you expect to get by?"

He handed the book back to me.

"Perhaps you should go back to your room," I said. I turned to put the book back with the others. "I don't mean to be rude, but——."

Before I knew what was happening, he had entered the cabin and come up behind me. In one swift move, he slid his arms around my waist, and I instinctively pulled away. I faced him to see that the gray eyes held something ominous now, a dark smoldering, and I felt my anger rise. "Get out!" I ordered.

He smiled and reached out to caress my cheek, but I grabbed his hand and yanked his fingers back so hard he cried out.

"Leave now," I said, "or I'll report you to the captain."

He just stared, his smile now vanished, and for one panicked moment I thought he might lunge at me. Instead, he brushed his arm across the bed so that all my books landed on the floor. "You can keep your precious books," he said. Then he left.

I closed the door behind him, my heart beating fast, and sat on the bed in the thin light penetrating the sea-drenched windows. At my feet, Luca's photo lay on the carpeted floor where the current of air left by Vincenzo's departure had swept it from the dresser. If it had creased with the fall, I think I would have run down the corridor and smacked Vincenzo, but it was unharmed, and Luca's large brown eyes that I had known since childhood looked up at me from the past. How I missed him! How I missed his presence in my life, his friendship, and the sweet promise of our growing romance before it was so cruelly cut short.

Behind me, the oceanic storm pummeled the glass. Pushing down an upwelling of despair, I tried to focus on the comforts of other memories, ones that did not include Luca and the void he had left. So I conjured up the view from the balcony of my house where the panorama of the town swept outward and below across the mountain, imagining how the town awakened to the coolness of an autumn day, my favorite season, when the stillness of the crisp air was broken by people roused to their daily business. I pictured my mother moving about the kitchen, the sleeves of her dress rolled up, her hands covered in flour as she kneaded the pallid dough to make bread in the early mornings of my childhood, the sky outside our window bleeding vibrant pink streaks into a cool blue, and for a short while I was taken away from the tossing of the ship, from the confrontation I had just had with that wretched young man, and from the violence of the rain pounding the decks.

Chapter Two

I avoided Vincenzo after the incident in my cabin. I would not allow his behavior to banish me from the dining room, but I was sure to choose my table close to the kitchen and the regular movements of the wait staff in their crisp white jackets. Walking the ship's corridors, I was constantly alert to the possibility that I would run into him, but Vincenzo did not bother me anymore, and I continued with my daily shipboard routine of reading and of studying English, which I knew I must master in order to survive in New York.

Late one night, after the storms had subsided and the ship once again rocked normally to the rhythm of the waves, I was awakened by the sound of moans and sobs and frantic, muffled conversation coming from the cabin next door. The cabin was occupied by a girl not quite out of her teenage years, pregnant and close to delivery, and her equally young husband. They, too, were from Calabria. We had exchanged pleasantries in passing a few times, although I did not know their names.

The girl's crying got louder as the cabin door

opened, then slammed shut. Running footsteps pounded down the corridor. I had assisted my mother enough times in delivering babies to know what was happening, so I got out of bed, slipped into my bathrobe, and hurried outside.

There was no one about. If what I suspected was true, the girl would be in no condition to answer my knock, so I called out first before trying the door. It was unlocked, left that way by her husband, I assumed, in his rush to get help.

I found her hunched over the bathroom sink, both hands pressed hard against its surface, with a terrified expression on her face and a pool of amniotic fluid at her feet. I helped her over to the bed.

"It wasn't supposed to happen yet," she wailed. "I thought I had time."

"It's not your fault. Everything is going to be fine." I adjusted the pillows beneath her head as she lay there whimpering. "Listen to me," I said, taking her face in my hands. "Calm down and take deep breaths."

She stared into my eyes, the tears on her face mingled with sweat. "What are you doing here?" she asked.

"I'm going to help you. It's okay, I've done this before."

After scrubbing my hands and pulling towels from the bathroom, I got her into position, gave directions, and did my best to calm her as she struggled.

Suddenly, the door swung open and her husband rushed in. He looked like he had just been relieved of a tremendous burden. "Anna, don't worry," he said. "The doctor is here."

Both the husband and the ship's doctor stopped short when they saw Anna on the bed, her legs spread, knees bent, and me in the act of examining her.

"Get out!" Anna shouted.

The husband backed away. As a man, it was not his place to be present at the birth, but Anna wanted both men gone. As the doctor placed his medical bag on the dresser, she turned on him. "Get out, I said!"

"Calm down," said the doctor. He looked at me. "I'll take it from here, miss."

Anna's panicked determination seemed to increase with the level of her pain. "No men," she cried. "No men." She was echoing the heartbeat of our age-old traditions, that the sacred mystery of birth, the most private and exclusive endowment of the female tribe, was the domain of women only.

"With respect, doctor," I said, "I know what I'm doing."

"I'm sure you do, miss, but I'm a doctor."

Maybe it was the confidence my mother had instilled in me, or maybe it was her influence taking some sort of mystical form, following me over the ocean and appearing when I needed it the most. Maybe it was my sympathy for Anna, hardly more than a child and so frightened, yet placing so much faith in me. Or maybe it was the boldness of traveling so far on my own for the first time in my life that made me brazen enough to confront that doctor. It didn't matter why. I would do it.

"I think you should leave," I said

The doctor frowned and flushed. He opened his mouth to speak but was interrupted by Anna's screech of pain.

Her husband gently touched the doctor's arm. "Please," he said, "let Anna have what makes her comfortable."

"Do you really want to leave your wife in the

hands of this . . . this girl?"

The young man nodded, his eyes wide and pleading, as Anna screamed again.

"I can't." The doctor shook his head and came closer to the bed, but Anna shrieked louder, whether from fury or pain I wasn't sure.

"I can do this," I said to the doctor. "I would not attempt it if I could not."

With pursed lips and flared nostrils, the doctor turned to Anna's husband. "If you insist on being foolish, so be it, but you must call for me if there are any complications." He picked up his bag from the dresser and turned to go.

"I'll need something to cut the cord with," I said.

His face was stiff as cardboard, but he pulled a surgical scissor out of his bag and placed it on the bed beside me.

The young husband looked worriedly at his wife. "Please take good care of her," he said before following the doctor out of the cabin.

Two hours later, Anna delivered a baby girl. After making sure mother and baby were comfortable, I cleaned up the bloody, sticky mess of childbirth and went out to look for the father. I didn't have to go far; he was waiting outside the door.

"You have a daughter," I said.

He looked momentarily stunned, then took both my hands in his and wouldn't let go. "Thank you so much," he said, vigorously shaking my hands. "Thank you. And what about Anna?"

"She's fine. You can go back in now."

I left them alone, Anna and her new baby and the young husband whose name I didn't know.

I found out later his name was Roberto. He and Anna named their child Angela, for surely, they said, there had been angels aboard that ship who sent me to aid them in their hour of need. I was flattered. They wanted me to be the baby's godmother—me, a stranger to them—but I politely refused because they would be moving to Pittsburgh to live with Roberto's brother and sister-in-law. It was not practical, I said, but I would always remember them. I gave them the address of my father's home in Manhattan in case they were ever close by, and they gave me the address of Roberto's brother. I knew we would never see each other again.

Anna and Roberto had wanted their baby to be born in America to symbolize their grounding in their new life, and she would have been, if not for the storms that caused a delay in our passage. All of us on board had planned to be on dry land before Christmas, but a voyage that was supposed to have taken ten days stretched into thirteen, and still there was no land in sight. So Christmas came and went with little fanfare. The staff set up a large *presepio*, the Neapolitan Nativity scene, in the ship's lounge beneath a white silk banner with *Buon Natale* scrolled across it in red and gold script. I found myself drawn to it on nights when I couldn't sleep. There was a magic to the scene, as with all *presepi*, the tiny figures living out their make-believe lives in the miniature sculpted streets and buildings, with the miracle of Christ's birth happening somewhere nearby. Alone in the quiet late-night hours, I studied every detail of this little town. I shrunk myself down in my imagination to walk the twisting cobblestoned alleys as if I were once again in the familiar streets of San Vittorio.

The plague of seasickness caused by the storms had subsided with the return of normal weather, so that by the time Christmas Eve arrived the dining room was well seated for the Feast of the Seven Fishes. On Christmas Day, although there was a small celebration in the lounge after Mass in the ship's chapel, I stayed in my cabin reading and wondering how my mother and brother were managing back home, whether they were truly enjoying the holiday with Uncle Enzo and our other relatives or just going through the motions of ritual without me.

Finally, the following day put an end to our long-suffering voyage. On December twenty-sixth, fifteen days after leaving San Vittorio, I awakened in the early morning to a light showering of white drifting past my window, and by late afternoon, under a sky thick with rapidly falling snow, our sea-battered passenger liner entered New York Harbor. My fellow travelers and I swelled up from the interior of the ship and onto the decks as soon as it was announced that we were nearing the famous New York skyline. I looked for Anna and her little family but did not see them. I wanted to wish them well in their new life in Pittsburgh, but the weather was harsh and the baby newborn, too small to be exposed to the rawness of winter.

Standing at the railing, I pulled my black woolen coat close against the heavy snow that now covered the decks like a carpet of frozen cloud. Through the chilly haze, the Statue of Liberty stood undaunted, her colossal arm forever uplifted in welcome. I knew there were many on that ship who had waited a long time to see her. Most of them were smiling, gesturing, some even crying in their unfettered excitement. Beyond the statue, the buildings of the city anchored the horizon to the waterline and rose up like a jagged gray mountain. Its powerful looming presence grew larger as we approached, and my stomach tightened as I imagined being swallowed by this place.

Only after the ship had docked and I was faced with the logistics of disembarking did I ignore the discomfort. Stepping off the ship felt odd at first, the pier solid and unyielding beneath my feet. Odder still was the disfiguring onslaught of the snow—so different from the sugar-coating snowfalls in the mountains back home—sticking everywhere and deforming the shapes of everything it covered. Oddest of all, however, was the presence of the man who came forward to meet me, the man responsible for my existence but whose face and figure I knew only from a few old photographs and tendrils of memory.

I stopped walking. What do you say to a stranger who is your father?

Of medium height and build, he could have been any man in this city of so many men, but when he was within a few feet of me I saw in his face traces of what I saw in the mirror every day: thin lips, dark eyes beneath thick lashes, and an aquiline nose. He wore a gray coat and a gray felt fedora. Smiling, he held out his arms, and I wondered how he knew it was truly me, his daughter, he was about to embrace. The last time he had seen me I was only a child.

"Alba," he said.

I stood there mute, my suitcase in hand. He took it from me, placed it on the ground, and the next moment I was pressed against his coat, feeling the dampness of the snow-spattered cloth against my cheek.

My brain turned over on itself, the questions somersaulting. I wanted to ask him why he had stayed away so long, why he had not come back for us after the war. I wanted to know who he really was, who he had been before he became so settled in this unsettling city, and if he thought the money he earned here and sent back home was worth the time lost with us.

But the questions never made it to my tongue. I clung to him, the wet-wool smell of his coat oddly soothing.

"Let's go home," he said in the familiar dialect of our region. The sound of our language in his mouth was a comfort, but the word "home," the place that existed for me in the distance I had just crossed, caught in my ear like a windblown burr.

Outside the terminal I froze, my legs suddenly, inexplicably, unable to move. The snow had immobilized the city. The streets were choked with it, cars—so many cars—encased in it, impossible numbers of people staggering through it, and everything, everywhere buried and indiscernible. A man stumbled into me and excused himself, and I grabbed my father's arm while a flow of humanity swarmed around us. Panicked, I held on tightly as my father gently nudged me forward. I wanted to run, but there was nowhere to go. I was trapped here in America.

Chapter Three

I awoke the next day, Saturday, to the hum of powerful vehicles and the shouts of workmen calling to one another as they cleared the snow-crippled streets. My father lived on the top floor of a six-story apartment building, one of several in its own little community, all built of red brick. The window across from where I slept framed a sunny still life of tree branches arched in front of the apartment building across the way. Thick sheathes of white burdened the branches and the building's window ledges and rooftop.

We had barely made it home the night before. My father managed to find a taxi still willing to take fares before the streets became completely impassable. The driver took us as far as West 83rd Street before he decided it was a bad idea, and we walked in a shower of white the rest of the way to my father's apartment at East 102nd Street. Never had I been so wet and cold, my woolen stockings and sensible shoes soaked completely through. Never had my muscles felt so abused as we lumbered onward, our legs moving piston-like in the knee-high drifts.

My father kept glancing at me like a whipped puppy. "I'm sorry, Alba, so sorry," he repeated the whole way as I tried in vain to reassure him that acts of God and weather were not his fault.

My father's apartment had two bedrooms, and one of them was now mine. In the cold gray atmosphere of the previous evening, the flowered wallpaper and dim overhead light had seemed dingy, but this morning the room was warm and the walls brightened by sunlight. I stretched out on the generous mattress between soft, lavender-scented sheets and pulled the fluffy blanket down from my chin as I planned my day. The first thing I intended to do was make good on my promise to Taddeo and write him a long letter, but that would have to wait until after breakfast, as the tantalizing smell of coffee and sizzling meat drifted in from the kitchen.

I never expected my father to cook. It was not something the men of our town ever did. Even in times of sickness or crisis, when their wives were unable to feed them, they relied on daughters, cousins, and female neighbors to bring over food. In spite of my still-new shyness around him, I teased him as I made my way to the kitchen. "What's this?" I called out before reaching the doorway. "Has America made you into a chef?"

To my surprise, the person standing at the stove was not my father but a middle-aged woman. Tall and angular, with short blonde hair and a wide mouth, she turned to me, egg-spattered spatula in hand, and offered a dimpled smile. "Good morning," she said in English.

I stared. Who was this American intruder using my father's kitchen to cook herself breakfast? I had heard stories of the madness of New York, of unsavory characters and their dangerous ways, but this woman seemed neither crazy nor disreputable. She pointed to the table with the spatula. "Please sit down, Alba. Let me get you some coffee."

"Who are you?" I asked.

Placing a steaming, fragrant cup before me, she smiled again. "I'm Charlotte," she said. As if that explained everything, she walked back to the stove, portioned out two plates of scrambled eggs and what I would later learn to call "bacon," and set them on the table before sitting opposite me. "So," she said, "dig in."

I was still perfecting my English, supplementing with books what I had been taught while at school in San Vittorio, but I understood what she said. I just didn't know what she meant.

"Eat," she urged, still smiling.

That I understood. The food was tasty, and as I chewed I tried not to stare at her in my awkwardness. I felt I should know her, that somehow it was my fault I didn't. She offered no explanation as she munched on her bacon.

"Your father has told me all about you. He's so happy to have you here, you know."

I nodded. How could he tell you all about me, I thought, when he doesn't even know me himself?

"He's been looking forward to seeing you for a long time."

I understood most of her words, but responding was another matter. It was more difficult for my brain to convert the proper grammar and correct vocabulary words at a pace fast enough to keep up a flowing conversation, so I skipped the niceties and got straight to the point: "My father, where is he?"

"Oh, Giancarlo. He went out." She brandished her fork towards the window over the sink. "You can see it's not a very good day for anybody to be out, but a few of the stores opened up this morning, so he went to see if he could get a newspaper. You know, no matter what disaster happens, the press is always working. You've got to hand it to them."

I wondered what it was I had to hand to them.

"I barely made it here myself," she continued. "They're saying this was a record-breaking storm. I got stuck at my friend Mildred's place yesterday. She doesn't live too far, but getting back here this morning was no easy task, believe me."

"Do you speak Italian?" I asked.

She chuckled. "Oh, no, I'm afraid I don't. I guess your father is going to have to do some translating around here."

The sound of the front door opening signaled my father's return. Hopefully, he carried with him an end to this mystery.

The bottom half of his pants were wet with snow. He placed the newspaper and a brown bag of groceries on the table before leaning down to kiss the top of my head.

"Good morning, papa," I said. With him I would speak only Calabrese, even if Charlotte could not understand what I was saying.

Charlotte got up and prepared a cup of coffee for him. He was already seated with the newspaper in front of him, the headlines blaring out the snowstorm, when she set the cup before him.

She began emptying the bag and putting the groceries away. "You know," she said, "I have some pork chops in the freezer. I think I'll cook them for dinner tonight. Would you like that, Alba?"

I nodded and smiled politely.

My father lowered his paper and turned to me. "Alba," he said. "If there's anything you want, just ask."

"Thank you, papa."

"This is your home now. As soon as they clear all this snow and things get back to normal, I'll show you the city."

"Papa?" I pointed to Charlotte as she reached up to place a can of peaches on a cupboard shelf. "Does she do all the housework here?"

He nodded and went back to reading his paper.

Back in my bedroom, after taking a package of stationery and a pen from my suitcase, I sat at the small desk beneath the second of the room's two windows. This one gave a view of the street running up to First Avenue. The plows had cleared the roads, now bordered on either side by walls of snow. Somewhere over the white cliffs of buildings there had to be a Catholic church. I intended to look for it once the streets were passable. Already I was missing the *Chiesa dell'Assunta* in San Vittorio, its solid exterior welcoming all who approached it. It was the heartbeat of our town and a place of refuge for me whenever I needed peace.

As I put pen to paper to write to my brother, I didn't know where to begin. It would be easy to describe my time on the ship (although I would leave out the incident with Vincenzo) and the bizarre surprise of a paralyzing snowstorm, but how could I tell Taddeo about the father he barely remembered when I knew so little about him myself? My father was proving to be reserved in his communications. Between meeting me at the terminal the afternoon before and at the breakfast table that morning, he had hardly spoken beyond what was necessary. I had imagined spending the previous evening talking with him well into the night, until one of us looked at the clock and said, "Oh, my, look how late it is!" I wanted him to want that. Instead, he made us a dinner of leftover lasagna and a salad, prodded me to tell him all about my voyage and of our family back home, and then sent me to my room with a tight hug and a promise to make life in New York as comfortable for me as he could.

So I told Taddeo what little I could of our father and filled the letter with descriptions of things I knew he would like: the Statue of Liberty, the canyons and caverns of city streets and buildings, and the strange feeling of being surrounded on all sides by snow. After asking about our mother and Uncle Enzo, I signed it and placed it in an envelope to mail as soon as I could venture out of the apartment.

The day ahead turned out to be long and uneventful. My father, having finished reading his paper, spent the rest of his time settled back in an overstuffed chair in the living room listening to radio programs. When he invited me to join him, I eagerly accepted, so intrigued was I by the large wooden box with knobs on the front. Back in San Vittorio, where electricity had not yet arrived, there were no radios in our homes. Only a few families, my own included, had the hand-cranked Victrolas that provided our entertainment. I lay my head back on the green brocade sofa and closed my eyes, focused on making sense of the foreign words entering the room. From the sounds of creaking doors and suspenseful music, I could tell it was a mystery program, and after careful listening, I was able to figure out that a woman had been followed home down a dark street and that the police were looking for her murderer. This, I thought happily, would provide another way for me to learn English.

Throughout the day Charlotte did the housework. She dusted around my father and me, did the laundry, prepared our lunch and later our dinner, so that by the time evening arrived and she joined us in the living room, she looked tired and ready for bed. I didn't know where she lived, but because of the snow, I knew she would not be able to get home easily. My father must have asked her to stay, and that was why she was still with us since early that morning. Surely, no one worked such long hours, even in America.

I expected Charlotte to make up the sofa for my father and take his room for the night because my father, I assumed, would not allow a woman to sleep in the living room. He would offer her privacy. It was the gentlemanly thing to do.

Charlotte plopped down on the sofa next to me.

"Shall I move?" I asked.

She looked perplexed. "Why would you want to do that? You don't mind my sitting next to you, do you?"

"No, of course not." If she wanted to stay with us, who was I to stop her?

The three of us remained together for another hour or so, absorbed in the stories coming from the radio, until my eyes began to close and I got up to go to bed. Charlotte was also drifting off, but after I got up she made no move to make up the sofa for my father.

"Where are the sheets?" I asked.

Again Charlotte looked confused. "There are sheets already on your bed, dear. Do you want fresh ones?"

"Not for me, for my father." I pointed to the sofa. "You will sleep in the bedroom, yes?"

Charlotte, looking worried, turned to my father, who looked uncomfortable. He got up from his chair and motioned me to follow him out of the room.

After a short silent walk down the hall, he stopped before his bedroom door. "We both sleep in here," he said.

Now I was the confused one. "But papa, that's your room."

He nodded.

"But she's the maid," I said, incredulous.

"No," he said. "She is not the maid."

Chapter Four

My father went back to work on Monday. The city's transportation system was getting back to normal, so he was able to take an underground train called the IRT to Long Island City in Queens where he supervised a factory that made paper bags. I had barely spoken to him on Sunday. He tried to talk to me, to offer small pleasantries and ask about life back home, but he made no attempt to explain the presence of this strange woman that shared his bedroom. I didn't ask. I wanted nothing from him, not even his words. Charlotte received the same treatment. I spoke to her only when necessary, and my sentences were short and emotionless.

Yet for all my stubbornness, I knew I needed him. I was not sure how to navigate my life in America, and he was the only person who could help me. My mother, of course, had sent me here to climb beyond the limits of our town and its centuries of folk remedies to study nursing. She had talked about it several times over the past couple of years until it had become something real to me, a possibility not so far beyond my reach in a place where it was said anything could happen. Yet my mother, like me, did not know the first thing about life in America or how I would achieve this goal. I now wondered if she and my father had even discussed my future in their infrequent letters to one another. Had she told him of her plans for me, and had he agreed before sending the money for my passage? He had made no mention of it since my arrival. There was only one thing I was sure of, that my mother did not know about Charlotte or she wouldn't have sent me here.

I waited until my father had left for work before preparing to venture out into the cold and snow to post Taddeo's letter and take a proper look around this fabled city. Charlotte was in the kitchen when I went in to pour myself a cup of coffee. She sat at the table with a plate of toast and eggs in front of her and attempted another feeble smile when she saw me. I nodded at her. It was all she would get from me, all she had gotten since Saturday night. "Breakfast?" she asked.

"No, thank you." I spoke in English, but my tone was icy and barely hid my disdain. It didn't stop her from trying, though. She had been persistent in providing me with meals all weekend, even though I hardly acknowledged her and ate as little as possible.

I drank my coffee standing up, staring out the window so that I didn't have to look directly at her. Outside was a bright blue morning.

"Alba, I wish you would talk to me."

"My English is not good."

I gulped the coffee and went to my room to get my coat. On a chair by the bed was a new pair of fur-lined leather gloves and a wool hat, Christmas presents from my father. I put these on along with my coat and collected the American money left on my desk with a card showing the exchange rate between dollars and *lire*. My father, it seemed, had thought of everything. Everything except postage stamps.

Satisfied that I was properly bundled against the cold, I hooked my purse over my arm and was heading for the apartment door when Charlotte rushed towards me from the kitchen.

"You can't go out, dear. Your father forbids it."

"Forbids?"

"You cannot go. Your father . . ." She shook her head vigorously.

I shrugged, pretending to not understand. She took my arm, attempting to lead me away from the door, and I pulled it away with a menacing glance.

"You don't know your way around. Your father is afraid you'll get lost."

I smiled wanly and opened the door. The last thing I saw when I looked back was Charlotte's figure in the door frame, her mouth still moving in protest.

Outside, the snow-slicked city glinted white in the morning sunshine. The streets and sidewalks had been cleared, forming valleys among smudged white mountains. All weekend I had been confined to the apartment, its atmosphere as chilly as the outdoors, and it felt good to breathe in the fresh cold air as I walked down the block looking for a post office. I went as far as Lexington Avenue, then turned south and looked down into a vista that stretched ever onward towards the end of the city.

I had seen photos of New York and had read descriptions in my guide book of what to expect. The crushing anxiety I had felt on the ship's deck had subsided into an easy fascination over the past few days as I watched the city come to life outside the apartment's windows. But it was not until I was walking in the middle of it, among buildings piercing the sky and continuous parades of cars in all shapes and colors, of streams of humanity churning in and out among the stores and businesses, the theaters and restaurants, did I fully understand what New York City was. No longer was I looking out across the water to a skyline of concrete and steel, an observer about to scale an impossible wall. I was now inside, a tiny part of the swirling excitement that vibrated all around me, and for a moment I was not a girl from a small mountain town across the ocean but a pioneer on a challenging new adventure.

Each block I walked I was met with new sights, sounds, and smells: the street vendor selling hot ears of corn, the policeman patrolling the corner, the woman carrying groceries in a large brown bag talking to another woman who walked a tiny black dog on a purple leash.

I had walked for some time before I noticed from the numbers on the street signs that I had wandered a good sixty blocks from my father's apartment building. I was used to walking long distances in San Vittorio, where visits to friends and relatives often meant walking to another town, but I had never had to negotiate snow-encrusted streets before. Slowed by the snow and distracted by everything around me, I didn't realize until the sun was high in the sky that I had not yet located a post office. Unlike my father, I was not concerned about getting lost. I knew that most of Manhattan was designed as a grid, with streets running east to west and avenues north to south, and I was sure I could make my way back without catastrophe.

I was about to ask someone where I could find a

post office when a colorful array of postcards in a shop window caught my attention. Immediately, I thought of my brother. The one and only postcard my father had ever sent us, a glossy photo of the Empire State Building, was nailed to the wall above Taddeo's dresser. I was convinced it was the sight of that picture every night before going to bed that made Taddeo want to build things. The promise he had made to me when I left San Vittorio, to join me in New York and build skyscrapers, was not just the momentary sentiment of a sad-eyed boy. Taddeo was apprenticed to a carpenter, and he would use his skills one day to build in America. Of that, I had no doubt.

The shop with the postcards sold mostly candy, fancy chocolates in elegant boxes, and an assortment of mints, licorice, and hard candies in bright metallic wrappers. The postcards were displayed on a brass rack among the boxes and tins.

"May I help you?" The salesgirl came out from behind the counter as I browsed. I smiled and shook my head.

"Are you visiting from out of town?" She was perky and wore a bright shade of red lipstick.

"Yes. No . . . sorry . . . Here, I live now."

Her blonde eyebrows crinkled. "You mean you live here now."

I flushed. I had made a mistake.

"Well," said the girl as she went back to her place behind the counter, "let me know if you need anything."

I turned to the postcards but could feel the salesgirl eyeing me as I lifted first one card, then another out of its holder. Did she suspect I would steal one?

After choosing a panorama of the skyline at twilight, I brought it to the counter, then took a dollar out of my purse and handed it to her. She looked at me like there was something wrong.

"Don't you have any change?" she asked.

I didn't know what she meant. If she had said "pennies" or "coins" I would have understood, but "change" to me implied some kind of alteration, so I just stood there not knowing what to say.

After a moment, I turned to see another customer standing behind me with a small box of chocolates in her hand, a slim young woman about my age with auburn waves in a stylish cut, green eyes, and a sprinkling of freckles across her nose. "Give her back the dollar," she said, "and add the cost to this." She handed the box of chocolates to the salesgirl along with a dollar of her own, and I got my dollar back along with a smirk from the salesgirl. I felt like a penniless refugee at the mercy of foreign aid.

The girl with the green eyes glared at the girl behind the counter while taking her change and her purchase, then smiled at me and headed for the door.

"Wait!" I rushed out and stopped her on the sidewalk.

"Now I remember why I stopped going into that store," she said. "That girl is so rude."

"Miss, thank you, but I cannot—"

She stopped me with a wave of her hand. "My good deed for the day," she said. "I believe that if you do nice things for people, nice things will come back to you. What goes around comes around, after all."

I didn't know what to say. I couldn't repay her without coins, and I was uncomfortable allowing a stranger to pay for my postcard, even if it cost only a few pennies, so I just stood there staring at her.

And then she laughed. It was a bright giggle, and it made me smile.

"So who are you sending the postcard to?"

"My brother in Italy," I said. "I have a letter, too, but I must put a stamp on it. Do you know where is a post office?"

"Come with me. My hotel has stamps for sale, and they won't make you feel bad about breaking a dollar, either. You can even mail it there."

Her name, she said, was Peggy, and she worked the switchboard at a hotel on the corner of East 45th Street and Madison Avenue. She was on her way to the afternoon shift but had stopped at the store to buy chocolates for her little brother, who was home with a fever. Her chattering was continuous, a lively stream of words that cheered me over the course of a few blocks until she stopped walking. "Well, here we are," she said.

We stood in front of a solid brick fortress rising into the winter sky. I followed her through the glass doors and up the carpeted stairs to the lobby where guests and hotel staff moved purposefully about. On elegantly upholstered sofas and chairs placed on either side of the lobby and on the mezzanines above, women chatted and men read newspapers. Flowers in ceramic vases decorated polished narrow tables, and vibrant potted ferns flanked arched entryways. From the molded ceiling a clock hung suspended on heavy chains, and beyond that, a fully trimmed Christmas tree rose from the floor to almost touch the lower tier of a crystal chandelier.

"This is beautiful," I said as Peggy led me up a short set of stairs to the long marble front desk where staff in smart uniforms waited on hotel visitors.

"William will help you," she said. "William, this is Alba. She needs to mail a letter."

A young man with light brown hair and eyes the

color of sapphires looked up at us and smiled, showing even white teeth.

Peggy took my hand and patted it. "Well, Alba, it was nice meeting you. I hope to see you again some time."

And then she was gone, breezing past the elevators with their shiny brass doors and disappearing into one of the arched entryways, leaving me with a momentary sense of sadness, as if I had just made and lost my very first friend in America.

I handed William the airmail letter, its paper as thin as onion skin, along with the dollar that had been rejected by the salesgirl in the candy shop. After receiving a handful of coins and another flash of smile from him, I left the hotel and began the long, slow walk back to my father's apartment.

Charlotte was ironing curtains when I got there. She saw me from the entryway of the kitchen, where she stood behind the ironing board, but said nothing. I went immediately to my bedroom and spent the rest of the afternoon studying my *WPA Guide*. There was so much to see in this city, from the colorful avenues of Times Square with its gigantic illuminated signs, to the hills and lakes of Central Park, that green oasis sprawling through the heart of Manhattan. But first I planned to return the following day to further explore the area around the hotel.

Propped on my bed and absorbed in the book, I didn't notice the fading daylight until the windows darkened to an inky blue and I had to turn the overhead light on. It was so easy to just flick a switch, yet ever since I had arrived, this simple gesture held a fascination for me, as did turning on the faucets and flushing the toilet. Our house in San Vittorio had none of these luxuries. It was a solid house, built in a time lost to memory, and its thick walls offered comfort and protection. Its balcony was a place to spend easy afternoons playing cards with friends or eating our afternoon meals bathed in the Mediterranean sun. When that sun went down behind the mountains each night, it never occurred to me that lighting the kerosene lamps was an inconvenience. I never questioned the need to draw water from the well to fill our glasses and our baths, was never bothered by the act of pouring a pail of water down the toilet to flush it. That was our life, and I lived it happily. Yet here in America that life now seemed primitive, although I longed for it with a nostalgia I could not explain.

The aroma of roasted chicken wafted into my bedroom. I was hungry. My long walk had taken its toll on my belly, and for all my disdain of Charlotte, I had to admit she was a good cook. So when my father returned from work and Charlotte called out that dinner was ready, I turned the light off in my room and bitterly joined them in the kitchen.

The atmosphere was chilly, as it had been over the past two days, our silence at dinner broken only by an occasional remark and the clinking of china and silverware. Charlotte had given up trying to make small talk with me. My father, unobtrusive at the best of times, was more quiet than usual, and I suspected he was getting tired of my attitude. I didn't care. If I had an attitude, it was all his doing.

In that ugly silence, my anger rose. It bubbled up slowly as I glanced at the two of them, so smug in their devotion to one another, so that by the time I had finished my meal I wanted to do something spiteful.

I glanced furtively at them, first her, then him. They paid me no attention. My father's eyes were on the chicken leg in his hand. Charlotte stared past him, chewing.

"I was out today," I said casually in English. "I walked through the city."

My father lowered the chicken leg to his plate. Charlotte wiped her mouth on a napkin.

"I told you to keep her home," he said.

"I know, Giancarlo, but she was determined to go."

They spoke as if I were invisible.

"I wanted to send a letter," I said. "To Taddeo. Remember him?"

"If she goes out again, make sure you go with her," he said.

"She's a grown woman, dear. She got home all right."

"Please, Charlotte, she doesn't know her way around yet. I need you to keep an eye on her."

He reached his hand across the table and placed it tenderly over hers. This act, this small gesture of affection, caused a physical pain in my chest. I got up from the table and loomed over him.

"How can you not feel any shame?" I said in our dialect.

My father looked down at his plate.

"Does my mother know?"

His lips became a straight line.

"Answer me!"

A muscle in his face contracted as he slowly got up from the table to face me. "Go to your room," he said.

"Is this why you never sent for us? Because you were keeping house with this . . . this . . . whore!" It was a terrible word, and I spat it out without looking at her.

At that moment, I learned my father could lose his temper. His hand came down hard on the table, sending the salt shaker toppling over to an accompanying chorus of rattling dishware.

"You will not talk that way in this house," he said in a raised voice. "Apologize to her."

"Giancarlo, please." Charlotte did not understand our language, but our tone was unmistakable. She sat rooted to her chair, wide-eyed and lost.

"Apologize, Alba. Now!"

I rushed to my room and slammed the door. Across the distance of the hallway, I heard only murmurs of my father's conversation with Charlotte as I paced the floor in the semi-darkness, so distracted that I didn't even turn on the light. What could either of them know about the life he had left behind as my family struggled during those years of war? Here in this warm, comfortable apartment, the cupboards stocked with food, he had forgotten where he came from. This city—this country—was a fairy tale. It had none of the raw reality that scraped our lives back home. It was true that the money he sent gave us a better life than some, but when the war stopped all interaction and the seas became battlegrounds for warships, we had to make do with what little we had.

Perhaps the difficulties might not have seemed so bad if he had been with us. We might have faced the food shortages more easily, might have dealt more calmly with fighter planes in our skies, had we not been left alone. We had Uncle Enzo, of course, and he did his best to care for us, but Uncle Enzo had a wife and children of his own to provide for. No, we needed our father in our household. Taddeo, especially, needed him as he stumbled through adolescence, trying his best to face challenging times as a man and not a boy. One day, in particular, had tested his nerve and had nearly broken my heart with its unfairness, a day when my brother, at twelve years old, had been forced to do a man's job.

The war was still pounding its misery on Italy, but the Allies were making their way up the peninsula from Sicily. The Germans had withdrawn from the south and were already occupying Rome. We had watched them from our windows and balconies marching through our town and only breathed freely after they had passed. They stole as they went, and Allied aircraft strafed not only them but any Italians who happened to be in the way.

Weeks later, Taddeo had been talking and joking in the *piazza* with a group of other boys when an Italian military truck slowed and stopped beside them. The truck's flatbed was open, its ribbed arches free of its canvas covering. The driver remained in the truck's cab while a second man got out from the passenger side. He, like the driver, wore the uniform of the Italian Army.

"You," he said to Taddeo, then pointed to three others. "And you, you, and you. Come with me." He motioned towards the flatbed, where four shovels lay. "There are two men buried in a vineyard. Germans, killed down there." He nodded to where the edge of the road dropped off into the valley. "Get onto the truck, please."

They rode in silence, smelling the scent of sun-warmed earth rising up along the dusty road out of town. At the edge of the vineyard, the man got out of the truck and ordered the boys to dismount and grab the shovels. Two mounds of turned soil marked the spot where the German soldiers were buried. Taddeo wondered whether it had been the Germans themselves or the Italians who had buried them. It didn't matter. Someone had respected the dead, and the soldiers had lain there since in shallow graves under the dark, sun-scorched earth.

The boys sank their shovels into the dirt. For several minutes, the only sound was the sifting of soil, and then came the sudden, abrupt thump of metal hitting wood. As Taddeo loosened the earth around one of the coffins, a crude plywood box hastily nailed together, he staggered. Released from the soil, the reek of rotting flesh rose up like an assault. All four boys hesitated, unable to bear the odor, but the man ordered them to continue.

With the dirt cleared, they lifted the first coffin out of the ground. As they carried it to the truck, Taddeo realized with horror that it was leaking and that the greasy decay of decomposition was seeping through the cracks in the wood and into their clothing.

Barely able to breathe for the stench, the boys lifted the second coffin, dripping and foul like the first, out of the earth. With both caskets secure on the flatbed, they hoisted themselves up while the man got back into the truck next to the driver. Taddeo stood with his hands on the cab's roof, his back to the dead, grateful for the rush of fresh air on his face as they drove towards the cemetery on the outskirts of town.

At the cemetery gates, when the caretaker came out to meet them, the boys jumped off the truck and pulled the caskets onto the ground. The man told them they could leave after that. He offered them a ride back into town, but Taddeo hurried out of the gates without a backward glance, the stink of death still lingering in his nostrils.

That night, Taddeo refused to sleep alone. He stayed in my bedroom, his head against my shoulder, until the dawn brightened the horizon over the mountain. He had cried in the night and was ashamed, a boy among women who could not control his emotions.

Now, in this new bedroom, in this bright and lively city with its hurrying masses, I longed for my old life, because for all its rawness life in San Vittorio was still *my* life. It was a life where familiarity kept us bound to one another, where tragedies were met with compassion and grace by those who knew firsthand how misfortune burned, since poverty and war left no one in the south of Italy unscathed. It was the town of my childhood, where I had friends and relatives who loved me. My memories of Luca were there, too, even if he no longer was, and it was memories of him, of Taddeo, and of my mother that nourished me now. This father of mine, who until recently had been only a memory himself, had betrayed us. I owed him no allegiance. And even though New York intrigued me with its brash, polished landscape of manmade canyons waiting to be explored, it was not alluring enough to keep me if staying meant going along with this lie my father had fabricated as *his* life.

I stopped pacing and sat on the bed that Charlotte had made up for me while I was out looking for a post office. The window shades had not been lowered, and I had been pacing in the glow of the streetlamps seeping in from outside. In the pool of silver spilling onto the bed, I began to relax as a thought came into my head, and I knew what I had to do. There would be no training as a nurse for me here in America, no new life of prosperity in New York. I would return to Italy.

Chapter Five

Everything I knew about midwifery I had learned from my mother. For as long as I could remember, I had been accompanying her into the softly lit rooms of women in labor, watching as she deftly guided slippery new life into the world. When the women moaned and screamed in the agony of the birth pains, I helped by placing cool wet strips of cloth on their sweating foreheads. I drew water from wells under moonlit skies when the basin in the room needed refreshing, and when the cord had been cut and the infant delivered into the mother's arms, I helped clean up the blood and pulp of what was expelled in the sacrifice of perpetuating life in San Vittorio.

We were healers, too, practitioners of folk medicines dating to before the collective memory of the town. San Vittorio had a doctor. He set broken bones and treated the more serious illnesses, dispensing drugs transported from Reggio Calabria. But his cost was more than the townspeople cared to pay, even though they begrudgingly did when necessary. They preferred to call on us for more common cures, like the plant-based plasters and poultices that drew out infections and caused swellings to go down, or for the treatment of maladies caused by *il malocchio*, the evil eye.

All my life I had been cautioned against the dangers of *il malocchio*. I was taught how evil intentions could blow through our lives on a dark wind, how negative forces could cause illness and misfortune, emotional currents sent out like radio waves across space. It was spoken of plainly in San Vittorio, and it was common knowledge that only by invoking God and the saints could it be defeated.

I had first learned to perform the ritual of removing the evil eye the same way I learned everything else— by watching my mother. I was very young, perhaps six or seven, when one day a young woman, recently married and having just returned from a three-week visit to her in-laws in Naples, came knocking at our door. She was plagued by headaches, she said, severe, incessant headaches that had begun the moment her sister-in-law had laid eyes on her, and they continued without relief regardless of what remedies she took. The sister-in-law was an older woman, unmarried and bitter, always making unpleasant comments in the presence of the new bride. Whether or not she had meant to cause harm didn't matter; jealousy was a potent catalyst and did not need anyone's consent to attack.

My mother took her into our kitchen. "You sit here," she ordered, pointing to the table. She pulled out a ceramic bowl from one of the cupboards. After filling the bowl with water, she placed it on the table, and from a small pitcher she carefully poured one, two, three drops of oil onto the water. Instead of merging into a single dollop of transparent green, the drops dispersed on the water's surface, proof that the woman had been a victim of *il malocchio*.

My mother's lips moved in silent supplication to the Father, the Son, and the Holy Spirit as her hand came up to her forehead, down to her chest, and touched each shoulder in the Sign of the Cross. Her face set in concentration, she recited the series of prayers that would bring down the blessings of God and lift the ill intentions that had caused the woman's headaches. Later, after the woman had left, my mother took the bowl of water to the edge of town and sent it splashing down the mountainside.

These things—the curing of the sick, the delivering of new life—were the skills that had come down to me as a legacy through generations in an ancient place where our afflictions sought solace through the old ways. We were woven into those ways, and though my mother was still young, she would not live forever. Who, then, would follow her in the line of healers and midwives in San Vittorio?

Waking up now in my sunlit bedroom, with the previous night's scene in the kitchen still a potent spice in my throat, I resolved to be the one to take her place. San Vittorio needed me, New York did not. Surely my mother would have no objection to my returning when she discovered the situation she had sent me to. I would write to her later that day to let her know I was coming home, but first I had my father to deal with.

I waited until he had showered, dressed, and was about to leave for work before approaching him. It would be a quick conversation.

He was getting his coat out of the hall closet when I came out of my room. "I want to go home," I said.

His arm halfway through his sleeve, he stopped

and looked at me. "No."

"No?"

"No." He finished putting on his coat. "This is your home now. This was your mother's request."

I was stunned.

"You've only been here a few days, Alba. You don't know what's best for you. Your mother and I do."

Your mother and I do. He spoke as if the two were a couple, my parents teamed together in concern for my future. I just stared at him.

"Be nice to Charlotte," he said. "She's not the terrible person you think she is."

He kissed me on the cheek before closing the door behind him, and I was left standing there with a sickness in my stomach. I had no money of my own. I had no way to get home.

Back in my room, I sat at the desk and pulled out some stationery to write a letter to my mother. I wrote quickly, spilling my battered soul onto those thin slices of paper. I told her of my distress, of my loneliness and isolation in this house of my father's where a strange woman had greeted me and I thought she was the maid. I asked how she, my mother, could send me here to a man who had become as much a stranger to her as he had become to her children. Did she know about this woman? Did she send me here without warning so I could discover that my father had disgraced her? And if not, why not? She should have asked the right questions of a man gone for years at a time. She should have demanded answers in those short correspondences that arrived so infrequently at the post office in San Vittorio. I finished the letter with a flourish of accusations and a reminder of my suffering, chastising and blaming her, a four-page document of jumbled sentiments in a hurried scrawl, and then I burst into tears before crumpling the letter into a tight ball and throwing it into the wastebasket.

For the next quarter of an hour, I sat at that desk seeing nothing, my tears drying into salty tracks on my cheeks. For comfort, I began to hum a song from my childhood, a silly tune about a rabbit and a sparrow that Luca had taught me.

Luca. What would he have thought of all this? What advice would he have given me, lost in this overwhelming city?

He would have told me to find a way.

Out there, across the snowy streets, the city was brimming with young women earning their own wages. It was a frightening thought. I was not here long enough to know how to make my way in this new world, and though I knew enough English to get by, there was still much more to learn. The taunting face of the red-lipped salesgirl floated before me, and I cringed.

But I had spent fifteen days alone on the ship coming over here. I had survived the heartbreak of leaving my family and friends and the home I loved. I had fought off the advances of that villain Vincenzo, had overruled the ship's doctor and delivered a baby, and had managed to keep myself healthy and strong when everyone else on board that ship was falling ill from seasickness.

If I were to make my way home, I had to take some kind of action. I needed to take chances, and I would start by confronting Charlotte.

I found her making up the bed, *their* bed, in my father's bedroom. I couldn't stop thinking of her as an intruder, that this was still my father's home that she had somehow invaded and was allowed to stay like a stray dog invited in out of the rain.

She stopped, mid-tuck, when she saw me. We stared at one another for a few moments in a silent stalemate until she straightened up, wincing and breaking eye contact. "My back," she said. "It bothers me now and then."

"We can talk?" I asked.

She gestured towards the bed, inviting me to sit. I remained standing.

"I want to return to Italy. My father says no. You will talk to him?"

Charlotte sat on the bed and looked up at me, her face showing what I would have mistaken for genuine concern if I had trusted her. "Are you really so unhappy?" she asked.

"You will talk to my father?"

There was a long pause while Charlotte looked away. I imagined she was thinking of the unexpected mess my visit had brought, of my failure to accept her as a vital ingredient in my father's life and embrace their relationship with joy, or at least indifference. Did she really think I would not mind this living arrangement, with my mother back in San Vittorio left to care for herself and our family? Our life was hard compared to Charlotte's, even if we did share my father's money.

She turned to me again with the same look of concern. "He does love you, Alba."

"He does not know me."

"You're his child. His biggest regret has always been that he couldn't be a proper father to you."

It was his choice to stay here, I wanted to shout, but I would not discuss so private a matter with her.

"I want to go home," I said. "You will talk to him?"

Another pause, and I knew then that she would not help me.

"This is what he wants," she said. "I'm sorry, Alba."

Half an hour later I was on the street retracing my steps from the day before. When I reached the hotel, William was at the desk checking in a middle-aged man with a briefcase. I waited at a polite distance, but William saw me and smiled in recognition as he handed the man his room key. There was something about that smile that suggested comfort, like spending a cold evening by a warm fire. It made me feel less alone.

"Need to send another letter?" he asked.

"No, I want to see Peggy. Does she work today?"

He nodded, his smile slightly fading. "Peggy usually takes her lunch break at noon."

The clock hanging in the lobby showed almost eleven-fifteen. "Thank you," I said. "I will wait."

I settled into one of the plush sofas and spent the next forty-five minutes watching the life of the hotel moving and breathing around me. There was no lingering in this city, no idleness. Everyone had a place to go, and everything had a purpose.

At precisely noon, Peggy walked out into the lobby. She offered a surprised smile when she saw me and joined me on the sofa, crossing her slender legs and holding her knees in the most casual way, as if we were old friends chatting. "It's good to see you again, Alba. But I sure hope you didn't come to repay me for that postcard. I told you it was my good deed for the day."

"No, Peggy. I want to ask something of you."

"Oh, well, in that case, ask away."

"I want to work. Is there work here I can do?"

"You mean here at the hotel?"

I nodded.

She thought for a few moments. "No," she said, "there are no open jobs that I know of." She stopped and thought again. "Actually, how would you feel about working in a bakery?"

"A bakery?" I knew nothing about working in a bakery, but neither did I know anything about working in a hotel.

"Yes. My boyfriend, Bobby, has a friend whose father owns a bakery just a few blocks from here. The girl who works there just quit to get married, and now he's short-handed."

I had no idea how an employee's departure from a job could leave the owner crippled. I pictured the poor man with part of his hand deformed, but for the life of me, I didn't know what one thing had to do with the other. I was sure I had misunderstood.

"And the Santuccis, the owners, are Italian. How about that?" She smiled broadly. "So are you interested? I could take you there now."

I was interested, and I was sure my luck was about to change.

The Fig and Chestnut was a cozy little place tucked between a cigar shop and a grocery store. To the tinkle of a bell hanging from the door, we stepped into the warm scent of sweet confections and freshly baked bread. Several customers stood in line waiting to order from a woman behind the counter, while a large, round-bellied man in impeccable white slid a tray of cheesecakes into one of the display cases. This was Mr. Santucci, I discovered when Peggy introduced us. To my relief, there was nothing wrong with either of his hands, which he extended over the display case to take mine warmly when he learned I was from Calabria.

"I am from Puglia," he said. For Peggy's benefit, our conversation was in English. "You know, the toe of the Boot could not kick Sicily without the heel of Puglia to provide leverage."

I was not sure what "leverage" meant, but I got the point of what he said and was charmed at how he chuckled at his own joke.

Mr. Santucci clearly enjoyed conversation. After asking Peggy how Bobby was, he explained to me how his son and Bobby had been friends since childhood. He mentioned that his son had chosen, regrettably, to work for the city's transportation system rather than become a baker, asked if he could get us something to eat, or some coffee maybe, which we both politely refused, and kept talking until Mrs. Santucci, a woman as small as her husband was large, came over to join us after having served the last customer.

"Hello," she said, smiling.

"My wife, Bettina," said Mr. Santucci. "She's been handling the counter alone since Linda left."

"Actually, that's why we came by," said Peggy. "Alba would like to work here."

Mrs. Santucci looked at me as if assessing my ability to handle her clientele. "Have you ever worked in a bakery?"

"No," I said, "but I can learn."

She smiled, and I wasn't sure if she was pleased with my answer or if she was mocking it.

"And how do you feel about speaking to customers?" she asked.

"I know enough English. I can speak to them."

She hesitated. I could see she was mentally calculating my level of confidence in myself.

"I will work hard for you," I said.

Mrs. Santucci looked at her husband, who shrugged as if to say the decision was hers. "Well," she said. "I suppose we can give it a try. It will save us the trouble of finding a replacement for Linda. She left to get married, you know."

"Yes, I know. But I, too, will not stay long. I need money to return to Italy."

Peggy looked surprised. I hoped I had not embarrassed her.

Mrs. Santucci bit her lower lip and thought for a moment. "Well, at least we know you're honest." She glanced at her husband, who nodded. "Okay, then. Temporary is better than nothing for now. You will work Mondays through Fridays and half a day on Saturdays with Sundays off. The pay is forty cents an hour, paid at the end of your workday each Saturday. You can start this Friday, the day after New Year's."

After walking Peggy back to the hotel, I spent the rest of the day exploring the city feeling lighter now that I had a plan in place. I even felt more confident in my English. I knew enough to wait on customers, and the Santuccis could help me if I needed them to.

After wandering through the underground stores and marble hallways of Grand Central Terminal, I made my way across to Times Square and spent the rest of the afternoon captivated by its colorful lights and enormous signs. I stopped beneath the marquis of one of the many movie houses and was so caught up in the moment that I bought a ticket for *The Lady from Shanghai*. Inside the theater, surrounded by gilded columns and archways, under a frescoed ceiling, I sank, enchanted, into the plush seats to watch Rita Hayworth and Orson Welles find love and murder on the Panama Canal.

It was evening when I came out of the theater. I walked to Madison Avenue and, for the first time, took the bus uptown. The bus fare and the movie were extravagances I would need to do without if I was going to save money to get back home. But I had gotten a job that day, and I had done so with an ease I had not expected, thanks to Peggy. I deserved a small celebration.

When I got home, my father and Charlotte had already eaten dinner and were sitting in the living room listening to the radio. I went to the kitchen to fix myself something to eat. I expected Charlotte to come in and try to feed me, with my father on her heels chastising me for being out again, unchaperoned by Charlotte and arriving home so late. Instead, as I made myself a ham sandwich, my father came in wordlessly and sat at the table.

When I brought my plate over to join him, his face looked tight and pained. In his hand were the smoothed out pages of the letter I had thrown in the wastebasket that morning.

Chapter Six

It was strange. I had spent the past five days angry and resentful, yet seeing my father there at the table, his hurt so obvious, saddened me. He *was* my father, after all.

"She went rummaging through my trash, didn't she?"

"She thought it might give some insight into your troubles," he said. "That maybe if we knew better why you were so unhappy, we could help you."

We. I wanted no help from her.

"It was private, a letter to my mother. She had no right to take it out of the trash. I suppose she asked you to translate?"

"Your mother knows about Charlotte," he said. He laid the letter on the table and slowly smoothed its crumpled edges while I stared at him across the cavernous gap that had suddenly opened up between us. "She has known for years."

Was this another cheat, an attempt to tame my behavior?

"I don't believe you," I said, picking up my

sandwich. "She wouldn't have sent me here if she knew."

"This is not something parents speak about with their children."

I took a bite of my food and chewed, then dropped the sandwich onto the plate, barely able to swallow.

"Try to understand, Alba. Change can be very difficult for some people. I wanted to bring all of you here years ago, long before the war, but your mother didn't want to leave San Vittorio. She hoped I would return with enough money to make a better life for our family. We were not unhappy, your mother and I, but we were not madly in love, either. After Taddeo was born and I came back to America, well . . . I met Charlotte."

"I don't want to hear this," I said. My stomach had gone cold.

"Alba, please . . ."

I got up from the table and retreated to my bedroom before he could say anymore. This room had become my sanctuary, the door a barrier against him and Charlotte. I crossed the floor and back again, reaching far into my memory for any evidence, any subtle clue I may have missed in my mother's behavior indicating she had known about my father's abandonment of us.

And then I remembered a day in spring when I was about Taddeo's age and my mother and I were on the balcony of our home peeling tomatoes. It was one of the few times she had spoken about my father, and it had more to do with her parents than with her husband. She had been describing her father's garden, how the tomatoes there seemed to grow larger and juicier than anywhere else in San Vittorio. Giancarlo, she said, would often come to barter olives from his family's groves for those tomatoes. Each time he came, he would sit with her for several hours until, after a few months, he began making his intentions known.

They married on a warm June day in 1920. She was twenty-four years old and it was time. How long could she say no? It was not that Giancarlo was unkind, or that he was too old, or not handsome. He was none of those things, so there was no reason for her to refuse him when he asked her parents yet again for her hand in marriage.

It did not occur to me when my mother told me this story that her lackluster acceptance of my father's proposal was a reflection of the state of their marriage. Nor did it occur to me later, when my mother's wedding ring was confiscated for the war effort and she showed no remorse in giving it up. When two strangers came to our house one afternoon collecting gold from all over the region, my mother took the wedding band off her finger, handed it to them, and silently accepted the cheap metal replacement they gave her.

After they left, I watched her open a drawer in the hallway cabinet, toss the ring inside, then go into the kitchen to prepare our afternoon meal. She began pulling what she needed from the cupboards—a large pot, a cutting board, knives, spoons. The broad beans on the sideboard needed to be rinsed, the onions cut, and the pasta dough rolled out and sliced into long ribbons. She sat at the table with the onions and the knife and looked up at me leaning in the doorway. I was angry.

"So this is how they plan to win the war?" I asked. "With women's wedding rings?"

She said nothing. There was nothing to say. At the

time, I thought it was just my mother being practical in her usual way. Now I wondered if perhaps that ring meant as little to her as the cheap replacement, a symbol of a discarded marriage.

I waited for my father to leave for work the next morning before I came out of my room. Charlotte said nothing to me as I drank my coffee and ate the eggs and bacon I had allowed her to prepare for me. I watched her wash the dishes. She stood slightly bent, her narrow hips leaning forward against the counter.

"Are you in pain?" I asked grudgingly. She turned, looking confused that I had addressed her. I waved my fork in her direction. "Your back."

"Oh," she said.

Maybe it was because I knew I would be going home soon and her life with my father would then be nothing more than a bitter recollection. Or maybe the sight of her pain touched the healer in me. Or maybe I was annoyed at my mother for not telling me the truth about my father's other life. Whatever the reason, I offered to help. "I will clean the dishes," I said. "Go rest."

I was getting used to the unformed words coming from Charlotte's throat whenever she didn't know how to react. They came out as choking noises, little bits of sound she had to stitch together before offering them over to me. She smiled down into the soapy sink as she turned off the water, and I stiffened under her hand on my shoulder as she passed me by.

Charlotte did not rest for long, though. It was December thirty-first, and they had invited friends over for the New Year's Eve celebration. I spent a good part of the day in my room with my English books, but I heard her puttering about the apartment, cooking, cleaning, preparing. I suppose my small act of kindness that morning had emboldened her because in the late afternoon she asked me to put up the party decorations. I didn't mind. It was a pleasant, distracting chore, taping streamers up and tying clusters of balloons in the living room, dining room, and entryway.

My father came home carrying bottles of wine and champagne in a large brown bag just as I was tying the last of the silver and white balloons to the arm of a floor lamp. He looked pleasantly surprised. "The decorations look nice," he said. "I'm sure Charlotte appreciates the help."

When I didn't answer, he walked past me towards the kitchen, the bottles clinking against one another in the bag.

Around eight o'clock, the guests began arriving, a festive crowd in suits and smart dresses noisily peeling off coats and hats in the entryway, all smelling of perfume and cologne. I wore my favorite dress, an emerald green silk, accented with a faux pearl necklace my mother had given me as a Christmas gift before I left home. Charlotte had laid out trays of hors d'oeuvres and sandwiches on the dining room table and a selection of cakes and cookies on the credenza next to a coffee setup. The guests helped themselves to food while my father poured drinks from a cart in the living room. Soon the apartment was close with warm bodies and cigarette smoke. Wines and liquors swirled in crystal glasses, and jazzy tunes from the radio competed with the steady roar of laughter and loud conversation. I tried to remain in the background, standing off to the side to take it all in, but my father kept introducing me to people, and I was forced to smile and politely answer the questions they felt obliged to ask. What did I think of New York? How did it feel to see my father again after all these years? Had I ever seen such a blizzard before in all my life?

I told them what they wanted to hear as the women cooed over my "charming accent." One of them, a plump, pretty lady in a blue dress who cornered me in the dining room, pointed out that Guy Lombardo would be bringing in the New Year on the radio and that Mr. Lombardo's parents were from Italy, too. I raised my eyebrows as if this news were fascinating.

"His orchestra," she said, "plays every year from the grill room of one of those big hotels. I can't remember which one right now. It's a New Year's Eve tradition." She raised her glass of amber liquid (not her first, from what I could tell) and saluted. "Here's to Guy Lombardo and His Royal Canadians."

As she walked away towards the living room with unsteady steps, I wondered if the hotel where Guy Lombardo was playing was the same hotel where Peggy worked. I imagined a room with linen-draped tables surrounding a polished dance floor alive with elegantly dressed men and women. Peggy would find a way to leave the switchboard and peek in unnoticed to catch a glimpse of Mr. Lombardo and his orchestra. Or maybe she wasn't working at all. Maybe she was out with her sweetheart dancing at some pulsing nightclub, keeping an eye on the clock so they would have plenty of time to get to Times Square and watch the descent of the giant lighted ball I had heard about.

I was brought out of my musings by the lowering pitch of the party. Reverie gave way to loud murmurings and then utter quiet before a woman's voice, strong and sweet, rose in a clear, throaty rendition of "Blue Moon."

It was Charlotte. I watched her from the doorway

of the kitchen entertain her guests while they listened attentively, some smiling wistfully, some swaying to the melody. My father stood slightly behind her as if to support her but not overshadow her place in the spotlight. He was beaming.

When she had finished, the little crowd exploded in applause and begged for more. She obliged them with "As Time Goes By," her voice pouring over them like honey. I knew these tunes, although at the time I didn't know their names. They were on the records in my father's collection, songs that Charlotte sometimes played on the phonograph while doing the housework.

Charlotte bowed among the clapping and the hoots at the end of her song. She grimaced halfway down and tried to disguise it with a strained smile, but I could see she was in pain.

After someone turned the radio back on and the party resumed its pitch, I made my way to the credenza and helped myself to a slice of chocolate-frosted angel food cake.

"I hope you like it." The voice came from a woman in a crimson dress with a black bow at her waist. "I baked that one."

I took a bite. "It's delicious," I said.

"Charlotte can really sing, huh?"

"Yes."

"She used to sing professionally, you know, when she was younger. With a band. They made recordings for several years. I think the band is still together, but they had to get a new singer."

"Why did she stop?" I asked, genuinely curious.

"Well, she met your father."

"And he stopped her?"

"Stopped her?" The woman looked amused. "Oh, no, dear. She gave it up voluntarily." I must have looked confused because she offered an explanation. "Everything changed when she met Giancarlo. She wanted to make a home for him, and that would have been hard to do with her singing career."

I hadn't thought of Charlotte as someone with a life outside of this apartment, or that she might have had dreams and aspirations.

The lady in the crimson dress offered a final thought, her finger raised, before sashaying into the living room. "Love," she said, "causes people to turn corners."

And love, I thought, standing there with my cake in my hand, causes mothers like mine to push their children to turn corners.

Mr. Lombardo did not disappoint. His orchestra entertained us throughout the evening until my father's voice rose above everyone else's calling for quiet as midnight approached. The voices and laughter died down as everyone huddled into the living room to hear the countdown. With raised glasses, they called out the seconds until 1947 shifted into 1948 and Mr. Lombardo's orchestra broke into "Auld Lang Syne." I watched everything from the dining room. There were hugs and slaps on the back, kisses from the women, and a string of Happy New Years repeated from person to person. I watched my father take Charlotte in his arms, and then I left the party.

It went on for another couple of hours. I lay in bed facing the window, listening to the muffled merrymaking and trying to fall asleep. Moonlight and the light of streetlamps silvered the window shade and cast a cold glow into the room.

Midnight had come and gone in San Vittorio six hours earlier, but the festivities would continue until sunrise. The town would have been dancing since nightfall to the brass band set up in the *piazza*, stopping only to revel in the fireworks that burst the night sky into a flaming spectacle. Homes would have been cleared in a raucous throwing of old pots and dishes from windows and balconies. Our family— Taddeo and my mother, Uncle Enzo and his wife and children—would have enjoyed the celebratory feast the women had been preparing for days, including the lentils for wealth and good health served over pork sausage. Cousins and friends would have been visiting one another all night, spilling over into the *piazza* to mill around the bonfire until morning.

I thought my heart would break. At that moment, San Vittorio was a dream out of reach, a place separated from me by an immense ocean impossible to cross, and Taddeo and my mother were nothing more than flickering images existing only in my mind. The loneliness bore down on me like a vise. I was a stranger here. I didn't belong, and nothing was going to change that.

Chapter Seven

When Friday came, I awoke at six in the morning, bathed, put on what I considered suitable work clothes—a plain skirt of brown wool with a cream-colored blouse—and at seven o'clock headed for the bus stop. It became clear to me that I would not be able to walk to The Fig and Chestnut, as the distance was quite far and I needed to save my energy for work. No matter. I was earning a wage now, and the five-cent bus fare would not make too much of a difference in my savings.

I chose a seat by the window so I could watch the city passing as we rode. The changing scenery distracted me from my nervousness. I had never had a real job before, and now I would be working in a foreign country with its foreign people and foreign ways. But desperation breeds confidence. I needed this job, and I was determined to do well.

When the bus left me off on the corner of Lexington Avenue and East 42nd Street, I walked the few blocks to The Fig and Chestnut and was welcomed with a warm spicy scent as I entered. Mrs.

Santucci received me with a cup of hot coffee and a crisp white apron that covered my clothes from chest to thighs when I put it on. "The customers will be coming in soon," she said. "There's a lot to learn. I'll train you today, and tomorrow you'll begin waiting on the customers yourself."

She walked me around the bakery, showing me where everything was kept and tutoring me in all I needed to know for setting up, serving customers, and cleaning up at the end of the day. In the back room, where the baking was done, her husband stood at a large table mixing ingredients in an industrial-sized mixer and rolling out dough. The Santuccis had already been there for hours, and all around the room tiered racks held trays of assorted cookies, muffins, rolls, and cupcakes waiting to be iced.

Mrs. Santucci had already filled the display cases for the morning's sales. She showed me how to work the cash register, how to weigh cookies on the white metal scale, and how to properly package the customers' purchases. All day I watched the flow of people in and out of the shop. Most of the customers were regulars coming in for their morning rolls or lunchtime treats, or grabbing their evening bread for dinner on their way home from work.

Just as my workday was coming to an end and I had watched, trained, and helped all I could manage for one day, William from the hotel came into the bakery. He seemed surprised to see me, but I could tell it was a ruse.

"Alba," he said far too loudly. "I didn't know you worked here."

It was a lie. I knew a lie when I heard one and this one was not even well disguised. I was sure that Peggy, in her sunny, offhand manner, had mentioned it to him.

I smiled primly and nodded from my place beside Mrs. Santucci, who moved to take his order. William was clearly not a regular here. She did not treat him with the same casualness she showed most of the customers, calling them by name and asking about their families. When she asked how she could help him, he looked lost and glanced anxiously around at the display cases before pointing to a chocolate eclair. "I'll take one of those," he said.

"Alba," said Mrs. Santucci, "would you wrap up an eclair for the young man?"

"Oh, that's okay," he said. "No need to wrap it up. I'll just take it."

Mrs. Santucci handed me a napkin, then winked at me and retreated to the back room.

When I gave William the eclair, along with the napkin, he stood there holding it. He was the only customer in the shop.

"You would like something else?" I asked.

"Oh, no. This is all." He took a bite, chewed quickly, and swallowed. "It's very good." He took another bite. "I like eclairs."

I watched the pastry disappear, then took the napkin from him after he had wiped his mouth and couldn't seem to find the trash can that I knew was out of sight behind the counter.

"Well, I'd better go," he said. "I'm working the night shift."

"Will you see Peggy?"

"Uh . . . maybe. If I do, I'll tell her I saw you."

I thanked him as he left, glad he had come. It was nice to see a familiar face on my first day at work, as if in some small way this corner of Manhattan was becoming my own, if only temporarily.

That night at the dinner table, Charlotte asked how my first day of work had gone, and I found I could answer her without my usual irritation. The day had given me confidence. I had worked a full eight hours, had earned a day's wage on my own, and had come out the other end of the experience on top. "It went well," I said.

Charlotte looked pleased. "That's wonderful," she said. "Just wonderful. Don't you think so, Giancarlo?"

My father had not said a word about my job since I had told him about it the previous day. I had meant to tell him on the day I was hired, but when I came home that evening, the crumpled letter in my father's hand banished any discussion of it. The following day was taken up by the New Year's Eve party, so on New Year's Day I went cautiously into the living room to find my father sitting in his favorite chair reading *Il Progresso Italo-Americano*, the Italian-language newspaper.

"I have something to tell you," I said to the back of the paper.

He lowered the newspaper and pointed his chin towards the sofa. "Sit."

I sat. I wanted him to be happy for me. I wanted him to be proud. "Papa, I got a job."

He stared at me, his face unreadable.

"In a bakery near Grand Central Terminal."

"Why?" he asked.

"To earn money, of course."

"Why? You don't need to work. You can help Charlotte here at home."

"Is that what I'm supposed to do while I'm here? Are those the grand plans for me here in America?"

My father shifted forward in his chair. "Your mother said something about becoming a nurse. Get settled first, and then we can look into that."

"I already told you, papa, I want to go home. If you won't give me the money, I'll have to earn it myself."

He looked confused, as if I were speaking a foreign language instead of our own. "Why are you doing this, Alba? Why are you so determined to be difficult?"

I had come to see in the short time I had been here that my father was a patient man. He did not anger quickly, nor did he feel the need to reprimand or play the role of the domineering parent. There was a kindness to him that I couldn't help admiring, and I could see he was trying his best to provide a pleasant home for me. But I could not remain in New York just to please him. It was my life, after all.

"Papa," I said, "I don't belong here."

He took a deep breath, his expression a mixture of sadness and frustration. I knew I could be headstrong. I wondered if this was the kind of daughter he had expected.

So when Charlotte asked him if it wasn't a wonderful turn of events that my first day of work had gone well, he just nodded and continued to soak up his beef stew with a chunk of crusty bread.

I found out the next morning that the city's busses did not run as frequently on Saturdays as they did during the workweek, so I was twenty minutes late to the bakery. The first customers were already lined up for their morning rolls and muffins, but there were fewer of them than on Friday, and they seemed in less of a hurry. In fact, the whole pace of the city seemed less rushed, the tone of the streets quieter.

I hurried into the back room to get my apron, mouthing an apology to Mrs. Santucci as I passed the counter.

"Next time, just leave a little earlier," Mr. Santucci said as he offered me a freshly baked croissant off one of the trays.

After gobbling up the croissant, I took my place at the counter and began taking orders as I had seen Mrs. Santucci do it, pulling the cord on the number counter above the cash register, calling out the next number, taking tickets from the customers, and politely asking what I could get for them. All morning I reached for breads from baskets and wrapped them in paper, removed pastries, cakes, and cookies from the display cases and boxed them up with the red and white twine hanging from the wall dispenser.

I even lost my dread of the cash register when my first attempt to make change turned out successfully. On Friday it had seemed like a hulking monster of scrolled metal with menacing fingers that when pressed sent up tongues of numbers behind glass. This was the symbol of the Santucci's livelihood. If I made mistakes with the money, it could mean unintentionally cheating someone, and I could lose my job while letting the Santuccis down. As a schoolgirl, I had done well in mathematics, so figuring out the money system here in America was not difficult for me. It was the cash register itself I found intimidating. I had never worked a machine like that before, but I was proud of myself that I had mastered it so quickly. So by the end of my workday, when Mrs. Santucci handed me my wages along with her compliments for a job well done, I felt like I had been working in American bakeries all my life.

It was cold outside when I left the shop. Snow still clung to the streets and sidewalks, laying in white drifts against buildings and in alleyways. It did not deter the people of this city, though, who were out shopping, eating in restaurants, and filing in and out of movie theaters. The crowds were not as thick as during the week, but they still moved steadily over the sidewalks and streets to the beat of traffic, conversation, and laughter.

I didn't notice him at first, not until he called out to me. I had taken only a few steps outside the door of The Fig and Chestnut when that voice, the sinister lilt of his greeting—*buon pomeriggio*—as if he were singing it, sent a ripple up my spine. I recognized it immediately, although I hadn't heard it since my time on the ship. He leaned against a lamppost, hands in the pockets of his woolen coat, a brown cap pulled low over his forehead. He was grinning.

"What are you doing here, Vincenzo?"

"Oh, so you remember my name. How fortunate for me." He took his hands out of his pockets and spread them. "Well, this county is free, I am told, so I can be here or anywhere I like."

"How did you know I work here?"

He pointed to the grocery store next to The Fig and Chestnut. "I was making a delivery yesterday. As I was unloading the truck, I saw you through the bakery window. You were behind the counter wearing an apron."

I turned to go, to leave him there as I had left him on the ship, an insignificant incident in the story of my journey, but as I walked away, to my great annoyance, I found him walking beside me.

"What kind of a husband sends his wife to America to work in a bakery?"

I ignored him.

"There is no husband, is there?"

"Go away."

"Or what? You'll bend my fingers back again?

Don't think I've forgotten that."

When we reached the bus stop on Third Avenue and I joined the line of waiting commuters, he still would not leave.

"So, where do you live?" he asked, rocking back and forth on his heels.

"What do you want from me?"

"An apology, to start with, and then maybe a night at the pictures together."

"You'll get neither. Now leave me alone."

The muscles in Vincenzo's face tightened, and a chill gripped me as I recalled how he had turned on me in my cabin. Here was a man who hid his cunning behind false charm and who felt entitled to take what he wanted. *Un uomo cattivo*, I concluded. A bad man.

"Why do you dislike me so much?" he asked. "Am I that bad?"

"Do you really have to ask?"

He pursed his lips and looked away, but still he wouldn't leave. It seemed like we stood there for hours, statues on the street corner, before the bus finally arrived. For one awful moment, I thought he was going to follow me home, but as the line moved forward he stepped back to allow the other passengers to board.

I dropped my nickel in the farebox and took a window seat towards the front of the bus. Vincenzo remained on the sidewalk, hands in his pockets, nonchalantly looking around. So he knew that I worked at The Fig and Chestnut and that I was not married. He probably assumed I had no male protection, that I was alone here, and vulnerable. Well, he was wrong. There was nothing he could do to me in a city like this, with people all around, with the Santuccis at work and my father at home waiting for me.

I rummaged in my purse for a mint and sucked it angrily as the bus pulled away from the curb. When next I looked out the window, Vincenzo was gone.

Chapter Eight

In the following weeks, William came into the bakery almost every day, always during the slow hours, buying eclairs and lingering to chat. Sometimes he wore his hotel uniform if he had been working, but other times he had on street clothes, stylish pants and jackets with tasteful pullovers covering tailored shirts. He was always well groomed, with clean fingernails and neatly pomaded hair, smelling faintly of aftershave. Mrs. Santucci always had something to do in the back room when she saw him, scurrying off and leaving me alone at the counter.

I looked forward to his visits. Mornings before work, I spent extra time choosing my outfits, making sure that my shoes were highly polished and that my skirts and dresses were creased in the right places. I even bought a wine-colored lipstick at Gimbels department store because the salesgirl said it brought out the color in my complexion.

My conversations with William helped me with my English, which was steadily improving. He introduced me to new expressions and was amused when I crinkled my face in confusion, explaining that the "killer-diller" flavor of Mr. Santucci's pastries meant that they tasted great, or that having "a gas" at a friend's party meant that he had enjoyed himself. It wasn't long before he lost the awkwardness he had shown on first coming into The Fig and Chestnut. Our topics were light, conversations about food and music, the latest news, and what was on the radio. I found out he liked to read, and we shared discussions about our favorite books. I asked him questions about New York landmarks, and he asked me about my life in San Vittorio. He had been stationed in Italy during the war, and he had found it a beautiful country, the people warm and generous. He was naturally easy-going and polite, and one Saturday afternoon he asked if I would like to go to the movies with him.

We agreed to meet the next day to see *Sorry, Wrong Number*. It was a thriller, he said, based on the radio program. I insisted on meeting him at the theater because I didn't want to introduce him to my father or to Charlotte. This was a day I wanted to keep separate from my life in the apartment on East 102nd Street.

When I met William that Sunday in Times Square, he was waiting for me beneath the theater marquee, the tickets already purchased in his hand.

"You look nice," he said.

I smiled and turned my attention to the patch of pavement directly beneath my feet. I was never very good at accepting compliments.

Once settled in our seats inside the theater, William went back to the lobby and returned with popcorn and colas from the concession stand. Then the lights dimmed, and we were alone in a tale of deception and suspense.

It was a welcome escape for me to get lost in the

flickering celluloid images spinning drama out of shadows and light amid the smell of buttered popcorn. There was no Charlotte sharing my father's bed here, no Vincenzo spying on me from the back of a delivery truck, no pressing need to earn enough money to regain my old life. There was only a house-bound woman on the screen trying desperately to report a murder.

Halfway through the film, William put his arm around my shoulder. It felt uncomfortable at first, strange, as if his arm did not belong there, as if no male arm could ever belong there again because none had been there since Luca's. But William's embrace was gentle, and I found myself gradually easing into it.

Afterwards, when we left the theater and emerged into the early evening and reality, I allowed William to hold my gloved hand as we walked through the crowded streets. We talked in our usual relaxed way, and I tried to catch glimpses of him from the corner of my eye, hoping he didn't notice. I liked the crooked curve of his smile, the straight line of his nose, and the sound of his laugh. It rose from the deepest part of him and burst out so unexpectedly.

We passed a wide restaurant window showing long rows of tables inside jammed with people. "Have you ever eaten in an automat?" he asked.

I shook my head. I had heard of these places of food-dispensing machines manned by an army of waitresses behind the scenes, but I had never eaten in one.

"Let's go in," he said.

Inside, the walls contained hundreds of small windows holding everything from sandwiches and pies to platters of meats and vegetables. William handed me some coins and showed me how the food was released after turning a knob.

"You can get anything you want here," he said, walking me around the restaurant and pointing out the food categories. After making our choices—turkey and gravy with mashed potatoes for him, roast beef with peas and carrots for me—we found a table by the window where we could watch the traffic on Broadway as we ate.

"So much food," I said, looking around at the rows and rows of selections. I was thinking of my mother and brother back home, where there was not so much food. During the lean years of the war, hunger had become the usual dinner guest at the tables of most San Vittorio homes, but even now such a quantity and variety of things to eat were unheard of back home. It was an observation I had made when I first arrived in America, where supermarkets overflowed with goods and where restaurants lined the streets. Food here was in abundance, yet no one seemed to find this the least bit miraculous.

He stared at me, smiling, as I chewed my roast beef. A flush began to creep up my face, so I turned my attention to the traffic outside the restaurant window.

"You know," I said, "I imagined the city would be colorful, but I never thought there would be so many, many lights. It's like day here even at night."

"Do you like it? Do you like the lights?"

"I do. It's cheerful. In my town, the streets are dark at night. There are only the—how do you say it— kero, kero . . ."

"Kerosene?"

"Yes, the kerosene lamps that light our rooms. With the windows open, they look like small fires inside."

"I know," he said. "I remember. Oh, not in your town, obviously, but in the towns we passed through during the war."

It felt good to know he had been there, fighting to liberate us in the end. I held this information close to me like a secret. He had shared my landscape, had been there at the same time I had been, each of us not knowing the other existed. And here we were now, sharing a meal together in a world untouched by the bombs and destruction that had blighted Europe and left it sifting through the aftermath.

"You know," he said, "at that time, Times Square was a lot less bright. They used to reduce the lights—dim-outs, they called them—so that the city was not as easily noticed from the air. I wasn't here, of course, but I saw photos when I got back. For two years in a row, they didn't even drop the New Year's Eve ball at midnight. Too bright. Instead, they rang chimes and church bells. Not real ones, though. Recordings."

"But there was no war here," I said. "No air raids."

"It was wartime, Alba. We couldn't take any chances. You never knew what the Germans were up to."

I imagined the city dimmed of its splendor, a whisper of itself beneath a darkened sky. It never occurred to me that the citizens of America could know fear of a far-off war. They did not have bombs exploding their ports and cities into rubble, did not know the paralyzing chill of seeing a squadron of bullet-spewing planes gliding through the sky. Yet here they were all that time, preparing for destruction even as they moved unharmed through their daily lives.

William seemed to be suddenly aware he had

touched on a sensitive topic. His face became grave. "It must have been hard for you," he said.

"It was not easy, but we were not as unfortunate as some." I did not describe to him the thread of anxiety that ran through us all. It drew us together so that we existed as a single fabric, thickly woven yet flexible, because how could any single human function with the constant threat of death hovering over us? We lived, and that was that. "Our town is high in the mountains," I said. "We had nothing of value to bomb—no ports, no factories, no bridges or tunnels of importance."

"Still . . ."

"Yes. Still."

"But you're here now," he said in a lighter tone. "I'm sure your father is very happy about that, even though I know you miss your mother and your brother. Will they be coming over soon?"

I had never told William about Charlotte, about my father's life in New York that did not include a reunited family living happily in his comfortable apartment. I did not want William to feel sorry for me or try to make me feel better. Nor did I tell him that I had helped my mother deliver the babies of San Vittorio, the skill that had brought me here, because I would not be studying nursing in America after all. There was a lot I had not told William about me and my life, but there was one piece of information I felt it would be dishonest to withhold. "They will not be coming over," I said. "I will be going back."

He looked like I had just slapped him. "What?"

"I am not staying here."

"But you have a job here now."

"I work to save money. I need money to buy a ticket for the ship."

He looked lost. "Peggy never said. Peggy got you the job, but she never mentioned why."

I placed my hand on his arm. He sat stock still, his turkey dinner forgotten for the moment, and I felt a small remorse.

"Well," he said, brightening stiffly. "Then we'd better make the most of our time together while you're still here." He flashed his brilliant smile and turned the conversation to other topics. I noticed he did not finish his meal.

It was a short walk to the bus stop afterwards. William wanted to accompany me home, but I refused, allowing him only to wait with me until the uptown bus arrived. The Sunday evening crowds were trickling home, the weekend over, and we stood silently for a while watching other lives finding their ways to other places. When the bus came, I kissed him on the cheek. "Thank you," I said. "I had a wonderful day."

He stepped aside as I boarded but remained on the sidewalk until the bus pulled away.

When I got home a little past nine o'clock, I expected my father to meet me at the door as my key turned in the lock and demand an explanation of where I had been all afternoon and evening. I was usually home well before this.

As it turned out, he was not at the door, but when I passed the living room I heard him call my name. He was in his favorite chair reading the Sunday edition of his newspaper, while Charlotte sat on the sofa crocheting what looked like a doily. She looked up and smiled when I entered the room, but my father's face was stone. "What hour is this to come home?" he asked.

"It's not that late, papa. I went to a movie."

"Alone?"

I hesitated. "No."

My father lifted the paper back up to his face. As I turned to go to my room, he said, "Invite him here for dinner next Sunday. I want to meet him."

Chapter Nine

I lay awake that night watching shadows drift across my bedroom ceiling. My brain was crammed with shifting thoughts: the warm satisfaction of sitting beside William in the theater melted into the disquiet of my father's request and mingled with my resolve to return home, now slightly softened by the image of William's face and the feel of his hand in mine as we walked along Broadway.

My life had fallen into a fairly pleasant routine, working my job at The Fig and Chestnut and spending my evenings quietly at home reading, writing to Taddeo, or listening to radio programs. Sometimes I explored the city. I discovered that the neighborhood where my father lived had at one time been an enclave of Italian immigrants, a place where generations of our people had formed and nurtured a community designed to recreate the better parts of our life back home. Although the area had changed since then, I could still find Italian foods in grocery stores, where the owners of these and other shops still spoke our language. I discovered a church on 115th Street where the priest delivered the homily in Italian, and I began attending Mass on Sunday mornings. It was a pretty church, built, I learned, by the hands of Italian immigrants who raised it lovingly, brick by brick, in-between working their regular jobs.

My routine was simple, perhaps boring by some people's standards, but it provided stability for me and a sense of purpose. I was even getting along better with Charlotte, although I continued to avoid her as much as possible.

Peggy, to my surprise, had come into the bakery to see how I was getting along. Just fine, I told her. I was enjoying my job. I didn't mention my encounter with Vincenzo. He seemed to have lost interest in me, anyway, because he left me alone after that first confrontation on the street. I had made note of delivery days for the grocery next door. From behind the counter, I could see the truck arrive and even caught his eye once through the window. He smiled and blew me a kiss, but that was all. He never waited for me outside again.

So I was handling my life. I had a plan. If things were not perfect, at least they were not horrible, but now this request from my father sent a wave of apprehension into my quiet little world.

Unable to sleep, I got out of bed and went over to my desk to write a letter to my brother. I had been keeping my promise, more or less, writing to him regularly, if not every day. I did not write to my mother, partly because I was still upset with her for not telling me about Charlotte and partly because our correspondence happened through Taddeo. He conveyed the news from America to her, and through him I accepted my mother's greetings and good wishes. Taddeo was the common denominator, the pole by which the ropes of our separate lives swung.

I missed him terribly. He was always cheerful and kind, regardless of what darkness life threw at him, and I wished I could be there once again to shelter him. Of course, he never asked for me to watch over him. No boy wants to be guarded by his sister, so I was careful to simply be a bystander, someone who happened to be around in case I could be of some use.

One night, only a few months before leaving San Vittorio, I had even had to defy the police to protect him. The town had just settled into dusk when the two officers came to our house. I saw them from the window and followed my mother to the door.

"What's happened?" she demanded.

"We need your son," said one of the policemen.

"My son! What has my son done?"

"Your son hasn't done anything. We need him to perform a service."

Before she could turn to call him, Taddeo appeared at the door. The second man addressed him. "Someone's been shot," he said, and I could see from the look on Taddeo's face that he was remembering the dead Germans in the vineyard. "We need you to come with us."

There were no master carpenters in San Vittorio, only Taddeo, who, at fifteen years old, was apprenticed to a master builder in San Michele. Someone had to build a coffin for the dead man, shot in front of his home in the countryside. Taddeo was the only carpenter available to them.

I watched my brother reluctantly get his tools and follow the men through the streets towards the main road. In a rush, before my mother could protest, I grabbed my shawl and ran after them.

"Where are you going?" she shouted after me, but I

was already down the street and too focused on following Taddeo to answer.

When I reached them, the policemen ordered me to turn back, as I knew they would. I refused. I would not let my little brother handle a corpse alone, not again. "No," I said. "I want to come with you."

"You'll get in the way," one of them said.

"I won't."

"You cannot come," said the other.

"I'm coming. Perhaps I can help."

They looked irritated, but I guess it was too much trouble for them to argue with me because they said nothing further and continued walking.

"What are you doing?" Taddeo whispered to me as we fell behind them. "Why do you want to see a dead man?"

"I don't," I whispered back, "but like I said, maybe I can help."

"Help with what? He's dead."

"Do you want me to go back?"

Taddeo hesitated. "No," he said. "I'm glad you're here. But stay outside the house. You shouldn't have to see a murdered man."

As we walked, the soft shadows of twilight deepened and a pale moon came into view. When I looked back, I could no longer see the glow of kerosene lamps illuminating the windows of the town.

We moved in silence. Around us, the trees and vegetation were dark against the hills. The mountain was still, except for the occasional call of a night bird and the rush of breezes passing through leaves and branches. One of the men lit a cigarette and offered one to his companion, who accepted it with a nod. The walk seemed endless.

At a dry riverbed, we turned onto a narrow dirt

road leading into farmland. There was a farmhouse in the distance, a square single-story building standing alone on a wide stretch of land. As we got closer, I saw a white sheet covering something on the front steps. One of the men motioned towards it. "There," he said. "That's the dead man."

I grew cold, and the widening of my brother's eyes told me that he did, too. Taddeo told the policemen that if they moved one inch from him during this ordeal he was going with them. They smiled because they knew he was young and unused to such things. They did not know he had dug up two rotting bodies only two years earlier.

Taddeo and I both eyed the sheet as we passed, following the men up the steps and over the threshold. Any talk of my staying outside was forgotten.

Inside the house, a large wooden table dominated the far end of the room. A woman sat at it, her head in her hands, rocking back and forth and moaning. She did not look up when the four of us entered. One of the policemen went to her and laid a gentle hand on her shoulder. Still, she did not look up. He leaned towards her and quietly said something into her ear. When her hands came down, her eyes were swollen, her face wet from crying. She clutched the crumpled handkerchief lying in her lap, looked up listlessly at the officer, and nodded. She did not seem to notice there were three other people in the room.

The policeman headed to a back room and motioned Taddeo to join him. I followed right behind them. The other officer tried to block me at the doorway, but I pushed past him to be with my brother.

On the wall of the room, a picture of the Sacred Heart of Jesus hung over a heavy wooden dresser that held a votive candle and a statue of the Virgin Mary.

Across from the dresser was a bed, its stripped sheets piled in a corner. Together, Taddeo and the policemen removed the old mattress and leaned it against a wall, exposing the wooden planks of the bed frame. With his handsaw, Taddeo began dismantling the frame to make the coffin. There was no other wood in the house. We could hear the wails of the woman in the next room, whose moans had risen to piercing cries as the saw worked against her marriage bed.

Taddeo worked quickly, wanting only to leave, while I stood nearby in the shadows cast by the lantern. He fashioned the wooden planks of the bed into a long rectangular box, and when he was finished, he made it clear to the policemen that the job of placing the body inside it was theirs. Out of earshot of the woman, they laughed in low tones and teased him. They were joking with him because he was young and naïve and because the situation was so ugly that if they did not joke all four of us would fall under the dark spell of grief cutting away at the heart of the woman in the next room.

The murdered man was big—a tall man, and stocky. When the policemen brought him in, they found that the casket Taddeo had made was a few inches too short. Taddeo would not touch the body. With a few tugs and pushes, the policemen managed to force it in, and Taddeo nailed the coffin shut.

When all was done, one of the men told us to follow him outside while the other stayed behind. We looked one last time at the woman, still sitting at the table, whose sharp wailing had given way to a soft guttural sobbing. She did not look up. I wanted to say something, anything, that would have meaning, but I could think of nothing. She was a stranger to us. We walked out into the night, and the officer accompanied us home.

It seemed that Taddeo was forever being forced to deal with the dead, and it frightened him. He did not spend that night in my room. Instead, he sat up in the kitchen with the lamps burning and the window shutters open, as if to confine himself within closed walls would bring death closer. I sat with him. We spoke little and played cards. My mother joined us, and we had a soothing snack of bread chunks in warm milk.

Now, writing to him from so far away, I felt almost a physical ache across the distance. I knew what I meant to my brother, how he relied on my guidance when men and circumstances forced him to do what was most objectionable to him. He needed me, even if he never said it, and maybe I needed him, too, as validation of my usefulness. I wondered if he would be disappointed in me for returning home and spoiling his chance of one day joining me in New York to build skyscrapers. Maybe he would understand that the pull of my old life, with its sense of order and clear view of what was right and wrong, was stronger than the desire to stay away. I didn't know. What I did know was that here in America nobody needed me.

I finished writing the letter, a short account of the past few days, including the mention of William as a new friend, and sealed it before going back to bed. I didn't tell Taddeo about my intention to return to San Vittorio. I wanted to stretch out his fantasy of my life here a bit longer for his sake, and I didn't want to have to tell him about Charlotte, at least not yet. As far as Taddeo knew, I was here alone with my father.

William came to The Fig and Chestnut for his eclair the next day. I was a bit disappointed to see him because now I would have to invite him to the apartment to meet Charlotte and my father. The bakery, William, Peggy—they were all a life apart for me, a second life in New York that included only my small victories. I did not want to mix them with the disappointment of my family circumstances. And since this was all temporary, since it was just a matter of time before I would be back in Italy, I didn't see the point in letting William think this mild courtship had a future.

But my father had spoken, and I suspected it would just be easier to obey him this time.

After serving William his eclair, I launched right in. "Would you like to come for dinner on Sunday? My father asked me to invite you. He would like to meet you." I wanted William to know this was not my idea. I also hoped my father's request would scare him off, but he grinned broadly.

"Sure. Great. I'd love to."

"Good," I said, hoping my disappointment didn't show. I wrote down the address on a pad by the cash register and gave it to him. "Three o'clock?"

"Sure."

"We eat early on Sundays."

"I'll be there."

For the first time, William did not eat his eclair in the bakery. He carried it out with him without further conversation as I watched the back of his coat exit through the door.

Now I would have to cook. I hadn't cooked a single meal since arriving here, and now I would have to plan a menu, shop for the food, and prepare it all myself, because I was sure that William, as my guest, would expect me to. I knew Charlotte would try to help. She was forever trying to ingratiate herself with me, and I didn't know if it was because she genuinely wanted us to have a relationship or because she just wanted to keep a peaceful home. She would offer to shop for groceries or even do the cooking herself, but I didn't need her. I had grown used to her, to her presence in my father's life, but I was not willing to embrace her. She was also still suffering from back pain, and although I was not fond of her, I didn't want to be the one to aggravate a painful condition by allowing her to help me. I had watched her hobbling about the apartment whenever she had a flare-up, stopping the dusting and washing to lean against a counter or sit for a moment. At those times, I even took the dust cloth from her or carried the laundry, taking up where she left off so that she could rest, and she always accepted gratefully. I knew there was not much that could be done for a chronic condition like that, although it could be relieved. We had a remedy for it back home, but she took pills the doctor gave her. She didn't need my remedy.

I had almost a week to decide what meal I would prepare for Sunday, so I pushed the thought of it out of my mind and focused on the customers at The Fig and Chestnut that day. When my work was done, I left the bakery, stepped into the cold glow of the streetlamps, and headed for the bus stop.

As usual, while waiting for the bus, I glanced around the streets hoping to catch Peggy on her way to or from work. Aside from her one visit to the bakery after I had started the job, I never saw her again, even though the hotel was not far away. It was as if she were my personal angel sent to help me and then, after her work was done, disappear. I often asked William about her, but the two were not as close friends as I had thought. All he ever said was that yes, he saw her around the hotel, yes, he told her I had been asking for her, and yes, she sent her regards. Peggy was like a butterfly, it seemed, colorful and airy, always fluttering about and always moving away whenever anyone got too close. Still, I kept hoping to see her.

When the bus pulled up to the curb and I moved along to board with the other passengers, I didn't notice who had joined the end of the line. It wasn't until I was already seated that I saw him get on the bus and walk to the back with a smile and a wink. My stomach sank. Vincenzo was following me home.

As the bus glided up Third Avenue in the afternoon traffic, I stared ahead, not wanting to turn around for fear of encouraging him. For some wicked reason, he delighted in making me feel uncomfortable. Was he really so intent on revenge for what I had done to him on the ship? Was his pride really so great? I knew there were such people in the world, men who trailed women, men who killed for spurned passions. Certainly, there was a strain of nastiness in Vincenzo, but whether or not he was dangerous I didn't know. It was possible that his presence on the bus was just a coincidence. There were still many Italians living in my father's neighborhood, so it would not be unusual for Vincenzo to visit relatives or friends uptown. Or worse, perhaps he lived in the neighborhood himself. Whatever the reason, if Vincenzo was truly a threat, I didn't want him knowing where I lived.

When the bus stopped at East 59th Street, I hesitated before hurrying to the front door and getting off just as it was about to close. I had hoped this quick, unexpected move would throw him off, but there he was on the sidewalk. He had exited by the rear door at the same stop.

I walked briskly along East 59th Street, turning around once to find him walking behind me, lagging about half a block. When I crossed the street, so did he. I quickened my pace, and he did the same. When I passed a small coffee shop, I slipped inside, hoping I had lost him in the crowd.

A waitress approached me. "Do you want a table," she asked, "or the counter?"

The last thing I wanted to do was sit for a cup of coffee. I was tired from work and wanted only to get home and take off my shoes. I peeked out the glass door but did not see Vincenzo on the street. "No, thank you," I said. "I have changed my mind."

The waitress turned back to her tables, and I went back outside. I scanned the street in both directions, but Vincenzo had vanished, so I headed for the nearest bus stop. I wasn't really afraid of Vincenzo. I knew he couldn't do anything to me on a crowded street. It was more of a spookiness I felt, an unsettling disturbance like spending the night in a graveyard—you know the dead can't hurt you, yet nevertheless, you jump at every rustle of a leaf, every hoot of an owl. That was Vincenzo to me, a ghost in waiting.

Something caused me to look back again, a small nagging in the back of my brain—my mother would have said it was the angels talking to me—and I saw him. He had concealed himself, which was not difficult in a city as bustling as this, with any number of doorways and corners to hide in, and now he was walking behind me again, keeping a distance between us.

I walked on, impatient to find a safe way home. All the anger I had felt for Vincenzo on the ship was now coming back, and I was about to turn and confront him when I noticed a policeman leisurely pacing the sidewalk in front of a barbershop.

"Sir," I said, "there is a man following me."

He looked past me, searching the crowd. "Show me who it is," he said.

When I turned, Vincenzo was gone.

The officer was sympathetic. Perhaps he had a daughter at home, or a wife. He walked me to the bus stop and waited until the next uptown bus had arrived and I had boarded.

When the bus reached my stop and I got off, I looked around in the pale light of the streetlamps, although I knew Vincenzo could not have followed me this time. Even so, his memory stayed with me like a whiff of acrid smoke as I hurried to my father's apartment building.

Chapter Ten

On Sunday, I got up early to prepare the meal my father had promised William. I had gone to the supermarket the day before, after work, to buy the ingredients. My father had given me money and told me to get whatever I needed. There was no restriction on food here, not in my father's house, not in New York, perhaps not anywhere in America. Although I saw people without homes on the street, asking for money and looking like their last decent meal was a long-ago memory, it seemed to me that if you had a regular job like my father had, and like I now had, you did not have to fear ever going hungry.

I waited until Charlotte and my father had eaten breakfast and retired to the living room, my father with his newspaper and Charlotte with her crocheting, before tackling the kitchen. As I set to work searching through cabinets and drawers for pots, pans, and utensils, I sensed someone watching me. I looked up to see Charlotte standing in the archway that separated the kitchen from the dining room. "Would you like some help?" she asked.

"No, thank you."

"Let me at least get the pans out for you."

"I said no. I do not need help."

"You mean you don't need *my* help." The emphasis on the "my" irritated me. If she knew I didn't want her help, why didn't she leave me alone? I continued searching the cabinets and pulling out what I needed, ignoring her.

"Alba, please talk to me."

"I am very busy right now."

She walked over and quietly placed a hand on the door of the cabinet above the sink, preventing me from opening it. I stared at the cabinet door, my impatience growing, then tightened my mouth and turned to her, my nose inches from hers. "What do you want of me?" I asked.

"I just want to talk."

She was not going to leave me alone. I would have to humor her if I was ever going to get this dinner cooked—the sauce alone took hours to simmer—so I walked to the table and sat down, gesturing for her to join me.

"Thank you," she said, sitting down opposite me. After an awkward pause, she spoke. "You know, Alba, you're making your father very unhappy with all this talk of going home."

"That is not your concern."

"Yes, it is. His happiness is my concern."

Who was this woman? Did she think her hold on my father gave her free access to dictate the life of his daughter? I wavered between fury at her audacity and amusement at her assumption that she could in any way influence my actions.

"My father remained in America," I said, "because that was best for him. Italy is best for me. His happiness is not my happiness."

Charlotte looked down at her hands stretched out on the tabletop. I was not sure if she did this to gather her most convincing words to influence me or to prevent herself from saying something unkind. I suspected she was reaching the limits of her patience with me.

"I know you're in a new place," she said, "and that takes getting used to. And I was a surprise to you, as well, wasn't I? Giancarlo told me you didn't know about us. But I can tell you for sure that he wants you here. He wants you in his home, and I do, too."

"So that he remains happy?"

"Yes . . . well, no, not only that. I just want you to know that you're welcome here, that your life here will be a good one."

"There will be no life here."

She looked away, and I suddenly realized from the expression on her face, a look of pity mixed with guilt, what was really going on in her head: neither she nor my father believed I would actually do it, would actually return to San Vittorio on my own. It was just a silly plan that would never materialize, the juvenile action of a child not getting her own way. Well, they could think what they wanted. I had arrived here alone, and I would return to San Vittorio alone.

"I must cook now," I said. "Please allow me."

Charlotte got up stiffly, holding the small of her back. "If you need me, I'll be in the living room with your father."

I did not need her. By nine o'clock the kitchen was laid out with an arsenal of cookware and assorted ingredients, and I began my work.

The dining room was set and the bread, what they

called here "Italian bread," with its delicate crust and soft white interior, was already on the table when William arrived. I was still in my bedroom when the doorbell rang, checking to see that my hair was in place and that I had not put too much rouge on my cheeks. My father answered the door. I had wanted it to be me, to be a buffer for William as well as for myself at this first meeting, but William was prompt and I was not. I walked into the hall to see William handing my father a bottle of red wine at the entryway and the two of them shaking hands.

Charlotte was already in the living room when the three of us entered. She greeted William warmly. "I'm Charlotte," she said, with no further explanation. What else could she say, that she was my father's mistress?

When we were all seated—William next to me on the sofa, Charlotte in an armchair opposite us—my father offered William an aperitif. "Sherry, vermouth, or Campari?" he asked.

"Uh . . . vermouth, please."

"It will open up your stomach to receive the wonderful meal Alba has cooked for us," my father said as he poured from the cart in the corner of the room. After he had poured drinks for all of us according to our tastes, he sat down in his favorite chair and raised his glass. "*Cincin,*" he said.

"Cheers," said William. He took a small sip.

My father wasted no time launching into a polite interrogation of William's life. "So," he began, "I understand you work at a hotel."

"Yes, sir. I work the front desk. Hospitality."

"Alba has told me almost nothing about you, you understand."

This was a reprimand to me. All week he had tried

to pry information out of me, but my answers to his questions were always brief. I offered only what I could get away with: that William and I had met at the hotel when I went there to post a letter, that he had served in the United States Army during the war, that his surname was Moone. I knew more, of course, like how William enjoyed reading poetry, how he loved animals and once had a dog named Rusty, how he wanted to work his way up to management at the hotel and save enough money to buy a home in Queens one day. I knew plenty about William from the conversations between us at The Fig and Chestnut, but these belonged to us, to William and me. I was not willing to share them with my father.

"And your father, William? What does he do?"

"He works for the telephone company, sir. Installations."

"William," said Charlotte, "do you live in Manhattan?"

"No, ma'am. I live in Brooklyn."

"Alba," she said, "maybe one day William will take you on a walk across the Brooklyn Bridge. It gives such a lovely view of the city."

"I'd like that," said William, turning to me.

I smiled wanly.

"I'm afraid," said my father, "that I haven't been very good about showing my daughter the sights of the city. It will be easier once the weather gets warmer and all this snow finally melts."

"It's okay," I said. "I understand."

"But she's been exploring on her own," he continued, as if I hadn't spoken. "And she has a job now, as you know." To anyone listening, my father's tone sounded innocent and straightforward, just a man stating facts. But I heard the disapproval in his voice.

It was another reprimand. "You see, she is earning money to return to Italy, even though we've said that her home is here now."

I was mortified. What was he up to? Did he hope that by bringing this up, William would persuade me to stay, or was he just punishing me? "Papa," I said, "William already knows this."

William looked down at the drink in his hand. "I would be sorry to see her go," he said.

"We all would," said Charlotte.

I got up and headed to the kitchen. "Dinner is ready," I said.

The smell of tangy tomato sauce followed me as I brought the large tray of lasagna to the dining room table. I had wanted us to eat in the kitchen, to keep things casual, but both my father and Charlotte insisted that the kitchen table was no place for a guest to eat. So I had set the dining room table with Charlotte's best china and crystal glasses and used her fancy silver spatula to portion out the lasagna and serve them all. My father poured wine out of a sparkling decanter, then refilled it from the bottle of Valpolicella that William had brought.

Throughout the meal, William gushed at how delicious everything tasted. I watched him eat with gusto, imagining how much he enjoyed the taste of my food in his mouth, the swaths of pasta and melted mozzarella sliding into the ricotta filling as he chewed. I had made crispelli, too, the rings of fried dough light as air, and calzoni, the half-moon mounds abundantly stuffed with ricotta, mozzarella, and sausage. Then came the braciole, the rolled slices of beef, with a side of mixed vegetables, followed by a green salad tossed in oil and vinegar to nicely settle the stomach after the meal.

While we ate, William told stories about amusing encounters with visitors at the hotel, and my father shared stories of his own about coworkers at the factory. They discussed politics and the state of the city since O'Dwyer took over the mayoral office from La Guardia. They exchanged ideas about music, books, and the latest news, and through it all Charlotte held her own, offering opinions and bits of information. I listened more than I spoke, which no one seemed to mind or even notice.

By the time Charlotte had helped me clear away the dishes (I could not argue with her in front of William), get the coffee cups from the cabinet, and bring the cookies and pastries, all nicely arranged on a silver platter, to the table, William looked overwhelmed. "I don't think I've ever eaten that well in my life," he said as I poured him a cup of coffee.

I was pleased, perhaps more than I wanted to admit.

"Alba worked hard on this meal," my father said.

I wanted to kick him under the table. There was no reason for William to know I had gone through any trouble for him. "Well, papa," I said, "I like to cook."

My father chuckled. "You do? You haven't cooked a meal since you've been here."

My face heated. I wanted to tape his mouth shut.

"Oh, Giancarlo," said Charlotte, "let her be. William, Alba's been very busy with work, you know. Giancarlo is exaggerating."

There she was again, trying to gain my favor, this time by lying for me. Well, I was glad for it, even grateful.

"William," she said, "how long have you been working at the hotel?"

And with that simple maneuver, Charlotte turned

the conversation away from my discomfort. At that moment, I almost liked her.

It was early evening when we finished eating. William and I went into the living room, while my father and Charlotte stayed in the kitchen playing cards to give us privacy. Free from any further embarrassments from my father, I relaxed beside William as we listened to a comedy program on the radio, his hand over mine on the sofa cushion. When the program was over, we listened to another and then a third before he got up to go home. By then, my father and Charlotte had already gone to bed.

"I had a really nice evening," he said. "I wish it didn't have to end."

I smiled and nodded. I had enjoyed the evening, too, but the hour was late, and I had to work the next day, and I was sure that the tingling in my chest throughout dinner had nothing to do with nerves. The way his lips glided over his words when he spoke, the rich tone of his laugh, how his eyes seemed to reflect a warm glow like the flickering blue of a flame—these were the things I had concentrated on when no one was paying attention. It was the first time my heart had moved since Luca.

I walked William to the door and got his coat out of the hall closet. "I'm glad you came," I said.

He grinned as he lowered his lips to mine. They were warm and soft, and I lingered in the first flush of this first kiss, hoping I would not be thinking of it when I boarded the ship to go home.

Chapter Eleven

Since we were children, Luca had always been the one to right the wrongs in our simple, predictable world. One of my earliest memories of him took me back to the classroom of our childhood. Something had to be done about our teacher, he said, because she had caused Matilda, the smallest and shyest of our class, an unbearable humiliation. She had caused the girl to wet herself in front of the whole class. No one laughed when it happened. It was a cruelty, a sting we all felt because it could have happened to any of us.

This teacher would not excuse us when we needed to relieve ourselves once class had started. Whenever one of us asked to leave the room, she always responded with the same tight-lipped answer to remain seated until recess. She did this consistently, with no exceptions. She was not old, so it baffled us that one so young should be so unyielding. Wasn't a young woman by nature supposed to be indulgent, as soft in her manner as an older sister, stopping now and then in the course of her day to dream of romance and how tender the feel of her young man's arm linked through hers as they strolled through the *piazza* on a warm, breezy evening? Our teacher was not such a woman. She was hard. So on the day that little Matilda could hold it no longer, she sent the girl home with a reprimand, soaked underpants, and no compassion.

Luca was so disturbed by this that he became sullen for days, and so he masterminded a plot to bring justice to Matilda. After class, outside the school, he gathered the boys together. They met in whispered conspiracy until a plan had been spun and agreed upon. The following day, when a small hand began waving in the air to attract our teacher's attention, and she replied with her usual curt dismissal, all the boys rose from their desks in unison and let loose their bladders, unemptied since the night before, onto the schoolroom floor.

Ever since that day, Luca was my hero. When there were fights in the schoolyard, I would be his champion, urging him on to victory over the other boys. If the teacher's ruler came down on his outstretched hands, as would sometimes happen when Luca's mind wandered off the lesson and over to the window, I would scowl and dart the evil eye in her direction. And if ever a girl would smirk at Luca's inability to answer the teacher's questions about history, mathematics, or literature, that girl would receive the bitterest scolding from me as soon as we had left the classroom and scattered out onto the street to go home.

Luca appreciated my fierce loyalty to him, and it was because of this that we became the best of friends. We spent our childhood happily playing in the town with the other children or having adventurous ramblings in the countryside until slowly, without noticing, we grew up, and our relationship transformed into a more mature version of itself. Luca remained my hero, but now the hero was less a St. George the Dragon Slayer and more a Sir Galahad with silken curls and bronzed skin. We were fourteen years old when he confessed that his affection for me had grown into something riotous and untamable, an aching tenderness he could no longer deny. I kissed him unashamedly then, and with gratitude, because he had voiced what I could not.

My father never knew Luca. Whenever my father's life in America was punctuated with his rare visits to San Vittorio, Luca was just another child among the many children of the town, a faceless boy running barefoot with the others, so my father could neither approve nor disapprove of Luca's place in my world.

But my father approved of William. He told me so when he came home from work the day after William's visit. I had gotten home from the bakery shortly before and was in the kitchen helping Charlotte set the table for dinner when he came in and gave us both his usual kiss on the cheek. "That boy," he said, "you should invite him here more often."

And that was it. There was no further discussion. I did not remind my father that this courtship was destined to end because I would soon be leaving New York. If he wanted to fool himself into believing otherwise, then I would let him. Arguing was pointless.

When the telephone on the small table in the entryway rang, it was William. "I'm sorry I couldn't make it to the bakery today," he said. "I got caught up at work."

"Caught up?" I asked.

William's soft chuckle floated through the

receiver. "I got busy. I couldn't leave the hotel, but I really wanted to see you."

A quiet glow pulsed in my chest, spreading fingers of light down to my belly.

"I wanted to thank you again for making dinner for me and to see if you wanted to go to the natural history museum on Sunday."

"Yes," I said. "I would like that." My *WPA Guide* listed the museum as a main attraction of the city, but even if it hadn't, I would have said yes.

"Great! I'll come by the bakery tomorrow. Oh, and say thank you to your father and your stepmother. I really enjoyed meeting them."

The warm glow chilled. "Charlotte is not my stepmother," I said.

"Oh . . . I'm sorry. I thought . . ."

"They're not married."

There was a momentary silence before William spoke, but I didn't hear what he said because I spoke over him. "I will see you tomorrow, William. Goodbye." I hung up before he could answer.

When William came to The Fig and Chestnut the following day, we talked as usual as if there had been no awkward moment on the telephone the previous night. We made plans for our visit to the museum, and when Sunday came I met him in front of the entrance on West 77th Street. "It looks like a castle," I said, staring up at the rough brick façade with its cone-topped towers on either side.

"I thought you would like it. That's why I wanted you to meet me on this side of the building. It's the most beautiful. So, what part of the world would you like to see?"

"What do you mean?"

"The whole world is here. We can visit Africa, Asia, or even outer space. We can even go under the ocean." He looked pleased with himself, as if he were my personal ambassador to the most exotic and fanciful places on the planet.

"You choose," I said. "I will follow you."

The interior of the museum was a vast network of interconnecting halls and exhibition spaces, each packed with animals and artifacts displayed in carefully designed dioramas.

"My uncle used to work here as a security guard," William said as we passed through a hall of forests on our way to the elevators. It was strange to see trees behind glass, even though William told me they weren't real. "I used to come here a lot as a kid."

When we got off the elevator on the fourth floor, the first gallery we entered contained dinosaur skeletons. I slowed my pace, awed by the remains of a gigantic creature whose body stretched impossibly long across the center of the room.

"Brontosaurus," said William. "Come on, let's get closer."

It looked like it could have been a beast from another planet or a once-living mountain with its long tail curving up to a massive back that flowed forward into a roadway of a neck. "How can this be here?" I asked. "How can these bones be here after so very long?"

"They're not bones, they're fossils."

"Fossils," I repeated. "*Fossile* in Italian. I understand. But what is the difference?"

And so William explained how bones became fossils, how the minerals in the ground replaced the bone over millions of years, and how only partial skeletons were discovered during excavations. "They fill in the blanks," he said, "when they put these things up on display."

I was impressed. "You should become a scientist," I said. "You know so much."

He laughed. "Doing this kind of work means spending months living in tents out in the middle of nowhere, digging under the hot sun for hours at a time. No, thanks. I like the comfort of the hotel. Steady hours, steady pay. A nice normal life where I get to meet lots of interesting people. Besides, I want to get married one day and raise a family. I wouldn't want to be away from home for so long." He looked away from me when he said this, towards the paintings of dinosaurs, fully clothed in dinosaur flesh, decorating the walls in their prehistoric habitats. I wondered if he did this out of shyness or because he didn't want to see my reaction to this revelation. He needn't have worried; I showed no reaction, though the thought of a future married William, with me long gone to San Vittorio, sent a tiny dagger of jealousy into my chest.

"Come on," he said. "There's a lot more to see."

William proved to be an excellent tour guide. As we roamed the exhibition halls, he pointed out the highlights, telling me the stories behind each, explaining how the dioramas had been recreated to represent actual places, how the animal skins were mounted on clay sculptures rather than stuffed so that they looked more life-like. He introduced me to minerals and precious gems, Mexican pottery and African masks, exotic birds, reptiles and fossil fishes, and the march of humanity from prehistory to the present day.

After two hours of exploration, we took a break and sat on a long circular bench that ringed a group of elephants mounted above us and ready to charge. It seemed sad to me that such majestic creatures should be destroyed for display. "Why did they have to kill them?" I asked.

"Actually, it's kind of ironic," he said. "All these animals were hunted for conservation."

Conservation. *Conservazione.* "That does not make sense."

"It's so people could see them and learn about them, and hopefully take an interest in keeping them from being hunted to extinction."

"Could they not teach without killing?"

"I suppose, but there's nothing like the real thing, is there?"

"Well, I think the museum hunters should have left these animals alone."

William took my hand and slid closer to me on the bench. Across from where we sat, a family of lions rested in the long golden grasses of the African savannah. Even from the distance across that large hall, I could see how skillfully the animals' muscles had been sculpted; they seemed about to ripple and contract with the next stalk and pounce. When I turned back to William, he was staring at his hand on mine, the tightness of his lips and the crinkle of his brows telling me he was struggling to broach what could only be a delicate subject. "Alba," he said after a long pause, "last night on the telephone I said something that seemed to upset you."

My hand went rigid in his. "It's hard to talk about," I said.

"You never talk about your home life. Why not?"

How could I answer that? How could I tell him that I was ashamed of the path my father had chosen, that my resentment of Charlotte had gouged a hole in my heart that was only now beginning to slowly close, not because I accepted her, but because my bitterness could not persist forever? "It does not feel like my home."

"It takes time to get used to a place, Alba, especially one that's so different from where you came from."

I looked up at the bellies of the elephants, those wild innocents destined to remain forever frozen in that giant mausoleum of dead animals, and something broke inside of me. I wanted to cry—for them, for me, for how I would hurt William when I left. Instead, I let my anger take control.

"How can my father live with that woman? He is still married to my mother. And my mother, she knows! Everything is all wrong. We were supposed to be a family again."

"So is that why you want to leave New York, because your father is with Charlotte?"

"Yes."

William twisted his mouth into what could have been a smile but wasn't and shook his head. "Alba," he said, "I think you're being selfish."

If he had struck me I would have been less surprised. "Excuse me?"

"Your father and Charlotte seem very happy together. They're not hurting anyone."

"They're hurting me!"

"Don't do that, Alba. Don't be a victim. Life is not a fairytale where we all get to live happily ever after."

My mouth opened, but nothing came out. Victim. *Vittima.* I was about to explode into a verbal avalanche, so I took a deep breath and stood up. "We are done here, William. I am going home."

He followed me as I hurried across the exhibition

hall, my footsteps echoing loudly on the hard floor. I wasn't sure where I was going, where the exit was, but it didn't matter. All I wanted at that moment was to get away from William.

"Alba," he shouted as the distance across the floor between us widened. "Wait!"

He caught up with me by a marble staircase and tried to take my arm. "Leave me," I said, yanking my arm away.

I rushed down the steps, but he remained behind, calling out to me. "I was only trying to help."

"To help?" I stopped halfway down the stairs and turned. William, at the top of the staircase, looked down at me with wide, worried eyes. "To say that I am selfish is help? To say that I am a victim is help? I don't need that kind of help."

I hurried down the stairs and easily found my way to the exit. Across the street, Central Park lay open like the enchanted forest of the fairytale that was not to be my life. I crossed over and slipped into the park, safely anonymous among the curving paths and arching trees, leaving the street, the museum, and William in the world of the other side.

Chapter Twelve

I avoided William the following week. He tried telephoning, but whenever my father or Charlotte called me from the little table in the entryway, I called out from wherever I was in the apartment that they should tell him I was not in. By the third time this happened, my father demanded to know what was going on. "Did he do something to you?"

I was sitting at the kitchen table, eating a bowl of pistachio ice-cream. "No."

"Then why won't you speak to him?"

"I'm not interested anymore." I could tell he didn't believe me.

"What happened?"

"Nothing happened."

"If he hurt you in some way, I want to know about it."

My father's tone was serious, protective, and I was pleased that he was putting my welfare above his fondness for William. Still, I was annoyed at being interrogated. "Papa," I said, "please just leave me alone."

He shook his head and walked out of the room.

By the end of the week, William came into The Fig and Chestnut to talk to me. I refused to do anything other than take his order, which he reluctantly gave so that he could stall for time. Fortunately, as soon as he broached the subject of our argument, another customer came in and I hurried to take her order, leaving William to stare after us before exiting the shop.

"Is everything all right?" Mrs. Santucci asked after William had left.

"Fine," I said, and I busied myself by tidying up the counter.

I continued to avoid him in the coming weeks, and he obliged me by not coming into the bakery again. It was now the middle of March, and I had saved quite a bit of my earnings. Soon I would have enough to purchase my passage back home. Yet there was Taddeo to think of, and my mother. I had been so intent on returning to San Vittorio that I had given no thought to putting aside any money for them. It was true that my father continued to support them, but I knew that my contributions would add to their comfort. William may have thought of me as selfish, but I was not. I would leave America with extra savings so that I could help my family.

I announced my plans at the dinner table one night. "Papa," I said, "I've decided to stay here a while longer, but I will be leaving in the summer."

My father's hand hesitated slightly while sprinkling a shaker of crushed red pepper onto his plate of pasta. "Yes?" he said, placing the shaker down after he had dotted his food with flakes.

"I want to have some savings to bring home with

me."

My father looked at Charlotte, who looked down at her food and poked at it with her fork. She did not understand what I had said, but my father's look told her it was the usual conversation.

"So you're no longer in a rush to go home."

"No. But I will go home."

"Maybe by then you'll decide to stay."

"I will not. I told you I want to go, and I will."

"Okay, we'll see."

The smugness of his tone angered me. "You may not want to help me," I said, "but I will do this on my own."

My father put down his fork and reached for the glass of wine beside his plate. He took a slow sip before placing the glass back down. He did this deliberately, looking intently at the glass as its bottom touched the tabletop. Then he ran a napkin over his lips and turned his full attention to me. "Alba," he said with a tolerance that suggested dealing with me was a trial that required patient endurance. "Stop this nonsense. You are not going back to San Vittorio. You have a nice home here, plenty to eat, all kinds of opportunities. What is wrong with you?"

"Wrong with me? You think there is something wrong with me for wanting to go home?"

And so it began, an argument in raised voices where neither side would give in and where Charlotte kept her mouth shut, expressing all she felt with the widening and narrowing of her eyes. It went on for several minutes until I left the kitchen in a huff while my father grumbled to Charlotte about the impossibility of my ever seeing any sense.

Silence tainted the dinner table over the next few

evenings. There was small talk, but it was strained and uncomfortable. It was only after I had finished eating and gone to my room that normal talk resumed between Charlotte and my father, a low muffled conversation that filtered along the hallway. On the third night, I answered a knock at my door to find my father standing there with his coat on, and mine, taken from the hall closet, draped over his arm. "Come," he said, handing me the coat, "let's go for a walk."

This was strange, a walk for no apparent reason on a cold evening after dark.

"Papa, I don't want to go for a walk."

"I insist, Alba. I want to show you something."

I put on my coat, my curiosity piqued, and followed him out of the apartment and down to the street.

"Spring is coming," he said, "and then you'll see how beautiful the city looks when the trees turn green and the flowers bloom."

I was quiet as we strolled down East 102nd Street towards the west side of the city. He, too, was silent, and we walked like strangers, side by side, under a crisp white moon that trailed the streets behind us. We turned north at Lexington Avenue, then west at 110th Street, past the northernmost edge of Central Park, and didn't stop until we reached another park nearby. My father led me through an entrance near a darkened pond, its water a black mirror in the still night air, and along a shadowy path towards a grand set of stairs.

"Where are we?" I asked. "And where are we going?"

"This is Morningside Park. The streets continue up there." He pointed to the top of the stairs. "That's where we're going."

For a moment, I was brought back to my mountain

home, where the streets were inclined and walking meant climbing, where every turn showed sweeping views across the valleys. Here, though, after reaching the top of the stairs, I saw only the rooftops of building in the dimly lit streets and a panorama of the park below.

We left the park behind us and walked where the streets continued until my father stopped in front of the entrance to a hospital. "You could take the bus here," he said. "It's not that far on the bus."

I wondered if there was something about my health he knew and was not telling me. The thought made no sense, but neither did this bizarre act of bringing me to a hospital and offering travel directions. And then I understood what he was trying to tell me. A sudden fear squeezed my stomach. It was true that he exasperated me sometimes. It was true that I still wanted to leave him. But it was also true that I had finally, after so many years without him, found my father.

He must have sensed my distress because his brows crinkled. "I'm not trying to force you, Alba."

The fist that was restricting my insides tightened. How could he think I would not want to be there for him? What secret had he been keeping from me? "Papa, whatever it is, you can count on me."

"Then you'll come?"

"Of course I'll come. I'm your daughter."

He smiled and grasped my hand. There was a glow in his eyes, a happiness that reflected in the light of the streetlamps, and I felt ashamed for having been such a difficult child. "For however long you need to be here," I said, "I will come every day to see you."

"See me?"

"Yes. Just tell me what it is, papa."

He laughed, then pulled me into a tight hug and kissed my forehead before releasing me. "There's nothing wrong with me, Alba. I'm talking about nursing school. Charlotte's friend Mildred has a daughter who became a nurse here, and she says they offer a solid education."

My stomach unclenched, and I lifted my face to the cold night sky.

"School?" I said up to the stars. I took my father's face in my hands and looked into his deep, dark eyes. "This is about school?"

"I told you I would look into nursing schools for you, and I did. There are others in the city if you don't like this one."

I lowered my hands and turned towards the hospital's lighted entrance. Behind that glass was a world of knowledge that I could only dream of, a place to learn the latest in modern treatment, to make a difference in the lives of countless patients, and it could be mine if I wanted it. "I'll think about it," I said, feeling the pull of temptation. "But for now, can we please go home?"

He nodded, and we walked back across town arm in arm as silently as we had come.

I spent the next two days wondering what to do with my life now that my father had laid this new path at my feet. There was healing in my bones, bred into me from my earliest years as a witness to my mother's vocation. Watching her soothe women in the deepest clutches of labor, a yearning had grown inside of me, year after year, birth after birth. I wanted to ease their suffering with my own hands, my own words of praise and reassurance as girls barely out of childhood, as well as seasoned women, bore down in agony. My mother's natural empathy and exceptional midwifery skills were renowned throughout the region, so young brides went to their nuptial beds knowing their future labors would be well attended. My mother had a gift, one that I coveted. She saw this in me, this potent desire to be of service, and she trained me with the same passion she doled out to the women under her care. Fear was not allowed in the birthing room, not for the woman in labor and not for me, the midwife-in-training. At the first sign of terror, usually coming at the onset of labor, my mother would remind her charge that women had been successfully carrying on the human lineage since time began and that this situation was no different. She soothed and massaged, coached and sympathized, but never would she allow the expectant mother to question her own ability to conquer. I had read once in a history book that the Aztecs considered women in labor to be warriors, and birth a battle. Ever since then, I saw my mother in the role of military leader, never allowing her warriors to fall.

When I turned sixteen, she allowed me, under her guidance, to deliver the child of a woman in a neighboring town. It was in the deep hours of a winter's night. It was also wartime, so a frantic knocking at our door at that hour could mean anything. To our relief, a slightly trembling young man stood outside, his hat in his hand, begging my mother to attend to his wife. He led us down our narrow street to a wooden cart attached to a pair of donkeys and helped my mother and me climb into the back. There were blankets on the floor, old but clean, and we bunched them up beneath our bottoms to soften the jarring of the cart when its wheels ran over a stone or a rut in the dirt roads. We pulled our coats close around us and tightened the knots beneath our headscarves against the waves of cold air coursing over the cart as it hurried along the mountain.

When we arrived at his house, the young man led us up a steep stone stairway and into a dimly lit room occupied by a small group of relatives. After scrubbing our hands in a basin in the kitchen, my mother and I followed the sound of soft feminine conversation to a bedroom at the back of the house, leaving the husband to join in the serious vigil of his extended family. A carved bed too large for the room cradled a girl not much older than I was, her legs spread on the covers. Her mother sat in a chair beside her, holding her hand.

I expected my mother to go to work immediately, but to my surprise she held back and motioned me towards the bed. When I hesitated, she made no move to help me.

"You know what to do," she said, and I did. The girl was in the early stages of labor, more frightened of the unknown than in any physical distress. Her husband had been wise to come for us so early. As her pain progressed with the passing of the hours, I held onto her, walked her about the room, rubbed her back as her breathing became heavy, and helped her over to the bed when she wanted to rest. All the while my mother watched me from a chair beside the girl's mother, talking now and then to the woman, but always keeping an eye on my movements.

Outside, darkness gave way to a soft light and the crowing of a rooster. Peddlers in the streets began calling out their wares, dogs barked, and townspeople awakened to their daily routines. The sun strengthened and sent slivers of gold through the shuttered windows. My mother extinguished the kerosene lamps and opened the shutters to let the warmth and freshness of the day into the room.

By now the girl was deep into her labor, and still my mother kept her distance. Her gaze never left me as I checked the dilations, monitored the contractions, and offered words of solace and encouragement while the girl struggled to breathe and push. When I saw the crown of the infant's head emerging, my heart skipped, and I called to my mother, who only nodded her assent that I was doing all the right things. Moments later the baby slipped out, and after I had cut the cord and placed the tiny boy into his mother's arms, I felt a surge of pride and gratitude like I had never felt before.

Now, so far away from the birthing rooms of San Vittorio, my father was offering me a chance to step into American medicine, a universe of science, knowledge, and equipment that San Vittorio would never see. This was what my mother wanted for me. This was the reason I was here. Yet I knew that in American hospitals, it was the doctors who delivered the babies. The most I could hope for was to assist. I hesitated over the tradeoff of surrendering the right to deliver over the education I would receive, an education that would far exceed what I had learned from my mother, and for the opportunity to serve greater numbers of patients. I was not sure if this opportunity was enticing enough to keep me here, to lessen my homesickness for everything I knew and had left behind, and for the compromise of accepting my father's betrayal of his marriage.

These thoughts consumed me over the next couple of days. I mused over them at night, staring at my darkened bedroom ceiling when I should have been sleeping. I carried them with me on the bus to and from The Fig and Chestnut and in the quiet times between customers during the workday. Mrs. Santucci noticed I was quieter, more reflective, and became concerned. I assured her nothing was wrong. I didn't want to discuss any of this. These thoughts were my own, the choices mine, and I would come to a decision in time.

Chapter Thirteen

On Saturday, William appeared at The Fig and Chestnut, startling me. His broad smile showed he had no apprehension, as if no falling out had occurred at the museum and I would be happy to see him. In truth, I *was* happy to see him, although I tried not to show it.

"So," he said, standing before the display case with his hands in his pants pockets. He wore a brown leather jacket, unzipped, and looked as casual as if he were about to take a long, leisurely stroll. "It's really good to see you, Alba."

I nodded. "Are you well?" I asked.

"Actually, I've been pretty miserable these past couple of weeks, but I'm feeling much better now."

It was difficult to look him in the eye, so I concentrated on the third button down on his shirt. "Would you like to order anything?"

"I would like to take you to lunch. I'll be back when you're finished with work, which I know will be in about twenty minutes, and then we'll go down to Greenwich Village."

He did not give me a chance to answer. He left

with another tinkling of the door's bell, and I stood there between the baskets of bread and trays of assorted cookies, unsure of how to react.

In the three months I had lived in New York, I had never used the underground train system they called "the subway." I preferred to ride buses or to walk, deliberately avoiding the subway entrances that stood on street corners like open invitations. Walking down the steps was like descending into a bomb shelter. Though San Vittorio, high in the mountains, had been strategically of no importance during the war and therefore spared the expenditure of explosives, I had heard of people in the coastal towns being trapped or killed in bomb shelters. They were haunting stories, enough to cause a shiver through my blood at the thought of going below the New York streets for any length of time.

I did not mention this to William as he led me by the elbow down the steps and over to the four-pronged horizontal wheel that served as the entrance to the trains. He handed me a coin to insert in the slot, then gently nudged me forward until I was pitched out on the other side, the trench of the railway just a few feet ahead of me. People of all sorts lined the platform: couples standing hand in hand, singles in smart clothes, old people, parents trying to keep their children from running around the platform, small knots of loud teenagers, even a beggar asleep in the corner at the far end of the platform. No one paid attention to anyone else. Their chatter, combined with the rumble of distant trains, unnerved me—a kind of slip of the stomach like falling in a dream—and I stood with my back to the wall as far away from the tracks as possible. William did not seem to notice my discomfort or he probably would not have made so many trips to the edge of the platform to bend over and peer down the black hole of the tunnel in anticipation of the arriving train. When it did come, he escorted me through the pushing bodies and onto the train, where we were forced to stand and hold onto a metal loop high above the heads of the seated passengers.

It was a short ride, and I was relieved when we left the subway and ascended once again into the clear sunshine. The landscape was different here; most of the streets had names rather than numbers and followed a maze-like pattern unlike the orderly grid system of the neighborhoods I had become familiar with.

I clung to Williams's arm as he led me through the afternoon crowds, along streets lined with low brick buildings, past cafés and closed nightclubs whose signs promised music, food, and drink when the sun went down. We came to a park, a wide expanse of concrete punctuated with areas of green and with a sunken circle at its center that looked like a pool or a fountain, dry now in the coolness of March. A Roman-style arch dominated the park's entrance.

"What is that?" I asked.

"That's Washington Square Arch."

"I did not expect to see Roman ruins in New York City."

"Oh, it's not really from Rome."

"I know," I said, and William's face reddened. I smiled, which seemed to ease his embarrassment because he continued with the same history lessons he had given me at the natural history museum.

"This site used to be a pauper's graveyard."

Pauper. *Povero*. "Poor people?"

"Yes. And they're still under there, thousands of skeletons. Do you want to walk through to the arch?"

"I would rather not.

He grinned. "Did I scare you?"

I was not a stranger to the idea of mass death. It had become commonplace in Europe during the war, a daily occurrence that we tried not to think about. No, my reluctance was not fear of the dead, nor was it an ambivalence to tread irreverently over a cemetery. I refused William's offer because I found such a place sad, a symbol of the invisibility of those unfortunate enough to have nothing in life, neither money nor family, no one to give them a proper burial. "I'm hungry, William. I would like to eat now."

"Sure," he said. "And I know just the place to take you."

William steered me towards the network of narrow streets that led deeper into the neighborhood, past row houses, shops, and small theaters until we came to a restaurant whose low-lit interior mimicked a grotto. The walls and ceiling were sculpted to look like rock, and soft blue lighting lined the perimeters. The waiter led us to a table beside a miniature waterfall spilling into a shallow pool of azure blue.

"This place is pretty," I said as we opened our menus.

"I hope you like the food. It's Italian. I hope it's as good as you're used to."

The menu items were written in Italian with a description below each in English. William asked me to order for us, saying he was sure to make a fool of himself by mispronouncing everything. The food proved to be delicious, with an antipasto of pepperoncini and olives, thinly sliced prosciutto and hard salami, succulent mozzarella and sliced tomato.

We followed this with plates of delicately seasoned seafood risotto and finished with glass goblets of tiramisu and cups of freshly brewed espresso. Throughout the meal, our conversation flowed as naturally as if there had been no interruption in our friendship. I was grateful that there were no uncomfortable pauses, no revisiting of where our words had gone wrong at the museum. That incident was ignored as if forgotten, and I was glad to see it go.

William paid the bill and we walked out into the cool sunshine, leaving the duskiness of the grotto behind us. "You know," he said as we strolled down the street, "I'm sure glad you changed your mind about seeing me again."

"Yes . . . well, perhaps I had been a little stubborn."

He chuckled. "Actually, I like that about you. You stick to your guns."

"My guns?"

"It's an expression. It means you believe strongly about something, and you defend that belief no matter what. But boy, was I glad to get that telephone call."

"Telephone call?"

"From your father. When he called the hotel and said you wanted to see me, I didn't understand why you didn't call me yourself. But I figured, hey, what's the difference, as long as you're not mad at me anymore."

I stopped walking. A thread of anger began to weave its way through me, and I stopped myself from saying anything. I turned to look at a pair of lamps in a shop window, focusing on the lavish embroidery work on the shades.

"Alba, is something wrong?"

I shook my head. "These lamps, they are rather

ugly, don't you think?"

William looked at the lamps, then at me. "You did know about the call, didn't you?"

"No, I did not."

"I'm sorry, Alba. I wouldn't have—."

"It's okay. I am not angry with you. I had a lovely lunch. Thank you, but now I would like to go home." I kissed William on the cheek and walked off to find a bus that would take me back uptown. He followed, taking my arm before I had reached the end of the block.

"I'll take you home," he said.

He looked so determined that I agreed, but the bus trip was awkward, one long stretch of silence punctuated with meaningless small talk. When it was over, I allowed William to walk me to the door of my father's building.

"I'll stop by the bakery next week," he said. "Is that okay?"

"Of course. I will see you then."

We parted with strained smiles and stiff hugs, and once inside the building I waited impatiently for the elevator, defiance pounding in my chest.

My father was dozing in his favorite chair in the living room when I came in, his newspaper spread upon his knees. I didn't know where Charlotte was or if she was even home. He must have felt my looming presence as I marched up to him because he jerked awake and looked at me with the uncomprehending stare of those suddenly roused from sleep.

"You called him?" I shouted. "You called him and lied?"

My father, now fully awake, shifted in his chair and looked up at me. "Alba, please listen to me."

"I don't want to listen. You had no right to

interfere. Do you think William can keep me here if I don't want to stay? You made a fool of me. He thought I was running back to him after he had insulted me."

I fled to my bedroom, slammed the door, and threw myself on the bed. When the inevitable knock came, I ignored it. He knocked harder. When I still didn't answer, my father's voice rumbled from the other side in a tone and volume I hadn't heard since the time I had called Charlotte a woman of ill repute. "Alba," he roared, "this is still my house, and you will open this door or I will remove it from its hinges."

I slid off the bed, dragged my feet across the floor, and opened the door.

"Your anger is your worst enemy," he said. "You had better learn to tame it if you want to have any peace in life."

He walked to the bed and sat down, then looked at me as he patted the space on the floral bedspread beside him. I joined him reluctantly, refusing to look at him.

"I'm sorry," he said, "I didn't mean to cause trouble. I just wanted——." He stopped, his forehead puckered as if remembering something. "What do you mean he insulted you?"

"It's nothing," I said, "Forget it."

"If he was not a gentleman, I want to know about it."

"William has strong opinions, that's all. I didn't agree with something he said."

"Oh, just a disagreement then."

I turned to him, annoyed by this new cavalier attitude. "Yes," I said.

"People will disagree, Alba. It's the nature of things."

"Why did you call him, papa?"

"Because I knew you wouldn't. Because I was trying to help." He placed his hand over mine on top of the bedspread and pressed it gently into the cloth. "Because he makes you happy, Alba."

How could he see this? Was I so obviously miserable that the only spark of joy he saw in me was when I was with William? I must be pathetic, a walking husk waiting to be filled.

The light from the window was fading, causing shadows to stripe the wallpaper. "I need to go for a walk," I said, "before it gets dark. I don't like walking here after dark. It gets cold."

He said nothing more as I turned my back on him and left.

The truth was, I was glad to have had the chance to see William again, but it should have been my choice to reach out to him, not my father's. I had missed our conversations. William had a way of describing things so vividly that scenes and people became real in my imagination, and this fascinated me. As a soldier, he had been to Rome, a place I had always wanted to visit. He told me about the Forum, where a walk in the sunshine sent him back to a long-ago market with toga-clad Romans bustling about their business just as their modern counterparts did on the streets beyond the excavated ruins. At least those ruins, he said, were not the result of enemy bombs. And he had found comfort in Italian churches, what he called "softly lit museums of faith." At St. Peter's, he reveled in the magnificent marble masterworks and ornate mosaics. For all its grandeur, the Basilica maintained a hushed serenity, even when it stirred now and then with the quiet conversations of people like him, outsiders awed by its stunning beauty. Whenever he spoke that way, whenever he allowed me to see something of my own country through his eyes, I felt a tug in my belly of wanting to go home pulling against the wish to remain with someone who could make me feel that way.

But William had no place in my future. The longer I stayed away from him, the easier it was to get along without him. My time with William had been pleasant, nothing more, and I carried this thought in front of me as I walked the streets of Manhattan in the crisp evening air.

Chapter Fourteen

The next day, I woke up early to attend morning Mass and slipped out of the apartment before Charlotte and my father were awake. I had come to an unspoken truce with Charlotte: she stopped trying so hard to win me over and I was less outwardly critical of her. She seemed to have accepted my resolve of not allowing any kind of warm exchanges between us, and that eased the pressure of having to avoid her annoying attempts at bonding. In a strange way, I respected her for this. I knew, in spite of my aversion to her, that her heart was not the ice chamber I tried to convince myself it was. In other circumstances, in an alternate life in which she had not attracted my father away from us, I might have even liked her.

Neither Charlotte nor my father attended Mass. I had asked my father once why he never went to church. I expected some profound reason, some inner rebellion against the authority of an established religious code, but his answer was far simpler than that.

"I get restless," he said. "I don't like sitting there

for so long."

As I entered the church that morning, I was well aware of my soul's duplicity, of the difficulty I had in softening my cruder emotions. I felt ashamed as I walked down the aisle in full view of the statue of the Madonna above the altar. She was holding the child who would one day preach forgiveness even as he took his last agonizing breath.

It was Palm Sunday. I slipped into my usual place close to the altar, absently stroking the strands of palm in my hand as the parishioners filled the pews. I was alone here. I had made no friends in this neighborhood, yet I had only myself to blame. I had fashioned my life around another locus, the world I had come to know as "Midtown." There, The Fig and Chestnut sat as a tiny reminder that our people could make it anywhere in this city, and there William's hotel offered a sweet familiarity whenever I passed it. Besides, sometimes the sound of our language spoken by people I didn't know, the smell of our foods coming from other kitchens, and the attempts to reproduce what we had all left behind made me homesick.

Some Sundays, waiting for Mass to begin, I would gaze in veneration at the statue of the Madonna and feel a longing for the *Chiesa dell'Assunta* in San Vittorio. Solid and welcoming, it was the heartbeat of our town and a place of refuge for me whenever I needed to escape. There was only one time when my sense of safety there was ruffled, and that was when I had gotten locked in. I was young, barely into my adolescence, when a missionary came to town. I sat in the front pew with my mother and Taddeo on one side and Luca on the other. At first, the man had my full attention, a stranger who had traveled from far away, speaking of salvation and grace with the flailing of his hands. But his praying and preaching lasted long into the afternoon, and my attention drifted to the corners of the church as his voice floated, disembodied, above and around me. I noticed small details in the church's interior: the tiny crack in the wall by the side entrance, the fineness of the lines forming the figures in the stained-glass windows, a mark on the tile floor shaped like a kidney bean. I heard the rustle of my mother's skirt as she got up to go home and prepare our dinner, and then all was as before. The voice at the altar ebbed and flowed, and my gaze once again wandered until the church and the people began to recede and a mind-numbing trance took hold. The last thing I remembered seeing was the crucifix at the altar, the late afternoon sun flowing through the side windows to gild its surface.

I awoke to stillness. Shadows had formed in the arches where sunshine had been earlier. On either side of me, Taddeo and Luca were sleeping, Taddeo's head on my shoulder, Luca's against the back of the pew, both with their mouths slightly open and emitting small breathing sounds. Everyone else was gone. When we found we were locked in, we shouted, faces pressed close to the heavy wooden door, until a passerby heard us and called for Father Nunzio to release us.

Sitting now in this church in New York, bodies fitted close together as we waited for the processional to begin, I recalled the freshness of the evening air that Sunday in San Vittorio as we crossed the *piazza* on our way back home. It was a freshness I had not yet experienced in America, a sweetness of still air fragranced by the breath of the mountain, by pine and earth and the unnamed flora hiding in the crevasses of backyard gardens.

A stirring at the back of the church and the opening strains of the organ signaled our collective rising and brought me back to the present. Because the rituals of Mass are carried out the same the world over, this was the one place in this foreign city where I could close my eyes and imagine I was back in San Vittorio. Here, following the familiar Latin from the opening prayers to the final blessing, and with the homily delivered in Italian, I could almost believe that the hard floor beneath my feet was built on Calabrese soil and that the votive candles flanking the altar were lit by friends and family whose homes I could visit after the ceremony. It was a bittersweet fantasy that always dissolved as soon as I walked out onto the concrete sidewalks of Manhattan, but it allowed me one tenuous link: I knew that as I sat in this church so far away from home, the sun causing the stained glass windows to glow with a heavenly light was at that very moment shining on the tiled rooftops of San Vittorio.

Once the processional had passed to the altar and the priest united the congregation with the Sign of the Cross, I sank into the comforting flow of ritual that carried me through to the end of the Mass.

Afterwards, I waited for everyone to leave before going to the stand of votive candles. Only a few people stayed behind in the pews, on their knees in silent prayer. I placed a coin in the brass donation box and lit my candle, only to find that I didn't know where to begin in my conversation with the sacred.

It was to the Madonna that I directed my prayers, perhaps because I needed the advice of a mother at that moment or perhaps because the imposing statue high above the altar, splendid in her golden crown and flowing robes, made it impossible for me to leave without addressing her. I stood in front of this rack of flames, each one signifying a private world of intimate suffering and joy, and realized that what brought me here was an intangible thing that had been building ever since I set foot on the pier of Manhattan. It had no shape, no structure where I could logically hang my reasons for needing help. It was an amorphous bundle of emotions sitting on my soul, and I poked at it, hoping to find a thread to pull.

I must have stood there for several minutes on the verge of frustrated tears when I heard the statue call me. It was a whisper at the back of my brain, but it was clear, a crystal voice singing my name. I looked up in amazement, only to find that the face of the Virgin was the face of a motionless doll. I must be delirious, I thought, or desperate, but when I closed my eyes to pray one last time, the thread came loose, and an outpouring of silent words fell from my lips.

I prayed for forgiveness for the ugliness I had shown my father. I knew he was only trying to do his best for me, a daughter he hardly knew, although he had only himself to blame for that. I prayed for the strength to forgive him for leaving us, and I prayed for the ability to overcome the anger that so often spiked my emotions. I prayed for my family back home, for Taddeo and my mother and all our relatives, that they be well and not suffer in missing me as deeply as I missed them. I prayed for William and Peggy and the Santuccis, that they be blessed and happy, and that William would come to understand why I would not be able to remain with him. I even prayed for Charlotte, that her back pain would ease and that I could learn to accept her, although I doubted I ever would. My prayers came out in an ardent flow, and I pictured every person I prayed for as distinctly as if they had been right there in front of me. It was a powerful release of captive emotions, and when I was through, I prayed for myself, for guidance, for some sign of where my destiny lay.

Before leaving the church, I took one last look at the statue in her lofty alcove. Her doll's face was lifeless, but I was sure the Madonna had heard me.

When I got home, I called William to tell him I needed some time away from him.

"I don't understand," he said. "What did I do, Alba?"

"You didn't do anything. I just need some time to think, to plan. Please respect my wishes."

There was silence, then a weak "okay," and I replaced the receiver not knowing when or if I would ever see William again.

Just then Charlotte appeared. She came out of her bedroom holding her purse and dressed to go out. "How was church?" she asked as she pulled her red woolen coat from the hall closet. It was almost spring here, but still people needed to wear coats.

"Fine," I said automatically. I always answered Charlotte this way when she asked how things went for me, how I was feeling, how my dinner tasted. Fine.

"Your father went out to get some fresh air. We're going to the pictures. There's some roast beef in the refrigerator if you get hungry."

I nodded, relieved to see her go. It was rare that I was home alone, and I relished knowing I would have the apartment to myself for the entire afternoon.

I went into the living room, curled up on the sofa, and closed my eyes. The stillness was comforting, and

I remained that way for some time, breathing in the tranquility, until a thought began to form in my head. I knew that thought was wrong as soon as it came to me. I had no right to invade my father's privacy, but I got up and went to his bedroom anyway.

I opened the drawer of my father's night table even as the guilt tried to stop me. (His night table was identical to Charlotte's, down to the matched lamps and the round-faced alarm clocks.) The drawer did not contain much. A small wooden box without a lid held a pair of gold cuff links and a tie pin. Beside it were several neatly folded white handkerchiefs and a packet of peppermints. That was all.

I moved to the dresser and pulled open those drawers. It was easy to see from the undergarments, stockings, and sweaters that the drawers on the left-hand side of the dresser belonged to Charlotte. I closed them without disturbing anything. On the right-hand side were men's socks and underwear, undershirts, and folded dress shirts. I touched nothing until I got to the bottom drawer where, instead of clothing, I found mementos. These I picked up and examined, careful to memorize where each was placed so that I could return the items without leaving any trace that they had been disturbed. I felt like a thief, but still I continued. All I wanted was a glimpse into my father's private life, the life I didn't know.

I lifted a small red case from the drawer and held it in my palm, almost afraid of what I might find when I opened it. Inside was a bronze cross attached to a ribbon of blue and white stripes, and somewhere in the back of my mind, in a place I had long forgotten, I pulled out a memory of knowing that my father had served as a soldier in the First World War. I ran my finger over the embossed letters, *Merito di Guerra,* and wondered what he had experienced on the battlefield to earn this medal. He never spoke of it. No one in San Vittorio ever spoke of that first war. And when this second war was over, the men of our region who had served never spoke of that one, either. Even here in America, with their young men returned from Europe and the Pacific, no one talked about the duties they had performed or the terrible things they had seen. Not even William. When he spoke of his time in Italy, he described the people he had met and the places he had visited as if he were on holiday and not fighting for his life and the life of the world.

After carefully replacing the medal, I opened a small leather case and found two passports, one Italian and one American. The Italian one had multiple stamps and bore a photo of my father as a younger man. A thin face smiled out at me, one whose expression held all the vigor and enthusiasm of someone on an adventure. The American passport was issued later. My father in this photo looked more like the man I recognized, older and more serious. I held the passports, one in each hand, as if weighing their value. Somewhere between the issuing of these two documents lay the severing of my father's ties to Italy, at least until he could bring Italy back to him. How could he have known that my mother would resist?

I placed the passports back in their case and put it off to the side, then lifted what felt like a picture frame wrapped in cloth from the bottom of the drawer. I thought it contained a photograph. Instead, I found a document stating that Giancarlo Domenico Giusto, whose image appeared in a small square photo above an embossed seal, was a citizen of the United States.

Beneath the frame was a folder, and inside were my mother's letters, thin crisp airmail envelopes with her name on the return address in San Vittorio. The last one had a postmark dating back to the week before I had left for New York. I shuffled through them, reading the postmark dates, getting a sense of the flow of their correspondence, but I did not go so far as to read the contents.

One last item remained in the drawer, a plain cardboard box. I pulled it out and lifted the lid. Mixed in with greeting cards and prayer cards decorated with angels and saints was a collection of photographs, each carefully labeled on the back with names and dates. There were a few of Charlotte and some of the two of them together in various backgrounds—parties at friends' houses, Christmas in the apartment, a day at the beach—but many were of San Vittorio. He must have taken them whenever he returned because they showed Taddeo and me at various stages of our childhood. There were infant photos, toddler photos, photos of a small me holding an even smaller Taddeo. We were in the kitchen of our house, in the street in front of our door, in the *piazza*. Sometimes we were with family and neighbors, other times alone in various activities: playing, getting ready for church, eating at the table on our balcony. There were even a few photos of my mother, a young Madolina, smiling and laughing, unmindful of the future that would break up her family. The last of the photos were labeled October 1935. There was a series of them, showing me at nine years old, a gangly girl with skinny legs, and Taddeo, with his round face and large eyes, at three. It was the last trip my father had made.

I don't know how long I sat there on the bedroom floor sifting through photographs and trying to remember his visits, unable to conjure up details of the things he had said and done when he was with us.

It was only when hunger for Charlotte's roast beef pulled me to my feet that I replaced what I had disturbed, hoping my father wouldn't notice the next time he opened the box that the photos had been rifled through. I didn't worry too much about it. How often do people look through old photos hidden away in a dresser drawer? It was enough for me that he had them.

Chapter Fifteen

Two days before Easter I received a card from Taddeo. It showed two little chicks sitting on a giant blue egg swathed in yellow and green ribbons with *Buona Pasqua* written beneath it in pink script. He had included a letter describing life back in San Vittorio: how his training in carpentry was progressing so that the master was now allowing him to install doors and window frames all by himself; how Nino, the doctor's son, had received a new bicycle for his birthday (the only one in town) and would not allow anyone else to ride it; how Valerio, our neighbor, had left for California to start a new life, and how his mother had wept for days after his departure. He ended it as he always did, with great love from him and our mother and with the hope that I would write back soon.

A lump of guilt swelled in my throat. I had stopped writing as regularly to my brother as I had promised him. Life in New York did not have the same easygoing pace of my life back home. I had fallen into a machine that manufactured a thousand distractions a day, and while Taddeo had to suffer my lack of attention, he never complained or chastised me for this in his letters.

I sat on my bed and ran my finger over the card. Part of the design was embossed, and as I felt the shape of the egg, the textured feathers of the chicks, I was transported back to San Vittorio, to when I held another Easter card sent by my father before the war. I had discovered it in a drawer in our kitchen. This drawer held all sorts of mismatched things: odd pieces of twine, ribbon, sewing needles, spools of colored thread. One day, needing to mend a hole in my dress, I looked in the drawer for a spool of white thread and a needle and came across an envelope tucked beneath a skein of red yarn. It held a small card decorated with flowers and brightly colored eggs. The printing inside offered Easter wishes along with a handwritten note from my father wishing us the same.

I didn't know what my mother ever did with my father's letters. I had always hoped she kept them in a box somewhere, maybe in her bedroom dresser, or anywhere but the trash can. I still don't know how this lone card had come to land at the bottom of the kitchen drawer, but the sight of it caught me off guard. It was as if a small part of my father had suddenly appeared in the form of words on paper, his thoughts solidified in the ink. I wondered then if I would ever see him again as I put the card back, any thoughts of mending abandoned, and walked out of the house and into the clear autumn day.

As I often did when I wanted to be alone, I wandered out of town to where the grasses grew long and the rough outline of the mountain sloped gently downwards in shades of green and brown. The war was still on, and in the distance, where the cannon were stationed, I saw soldiers. They could have been any group of townsmen were it not for the Italian military uniforms and the occasional flashes of sunlight reflecting off the metal of their weapons. Yet their presence there could not lessen my enjoyment of the land or take away the comfort of the dirt crunching under my feet as I walked about in the dry heat of the afternoon.

All I wanted was to walk, to find a sweet distraction in the way the streets gave way to rough roads and solitude. I loved the mountain. It was a living, breathing behemoth covered in a vast tapestry of humanity and nature living intertwined lives. At its foot, on the edge of the world, the Ionian Sea stretched clear and glistening into the distance, towards other lands, other people, and towards my father.

A shout caught my attention. Closer to the soldiers now, I saw they were agitated, and I realized I had wandered into a restricted area. One of them pointed a gun at me, calling for me to leave. I ran, and finding I had taken the wrong direction, stumbled farther into land not open to me. The ground sloped away in a gentle roll of yellow earth and dark grass. Olive trees grasped the hills in vast cultivated forests against a deep blue sky. The more the man shouted, the more I ran, confused, my legs heavy with trembling, darting across the soldier's path and coming within yards of his rifle. Blind to the uniform and the weapon, I saw only the blue of the horizon across the ridge of the mountain.

A hand grabbed the cloth of my dress at the neck. Trembling and sick, I turned to see the soldier gripping me, his face dark and sweaty.

"I could have killed you," he said. He was a

middle-aged man with small lines across his forehead. "Go." He released his hold on me. "Don't ever come back here."

And I didn't, not even after the war had ended and the soldiers had gone. Reports of live ammunition laying around for months afterwards, of children playing with it, losing limbs and lives, of a string of explosions blowing up a man with horse and wagon as he unknowingly crossed over a still-active land mine in a post-war period without order, without law, without knowing what would happen next—these things stopped my wanderings.

I have often wondered about that soldier, who he was and if he had a wife and children who worried about him. What had he felt when he saw me running, knowing it was his duty to shoot, even at me, a civilian and a girl? I hoped he had survived the war.

We spent Easter Sunday quietly at home. Charlotte had been confined to bed for most of the week with her bad back, so I cooked a midday meal of ravioli followed by roasted lamb and artichokes fried in olive oil. For dessert, I had brought home a pastiera cake from The Fig and Chestnut, which I served with coffee. My father had invited some of his male friends to come over later in the day to play cards and drink wine at the dining room table. By the time they arrived, Charlotte had gone back to bed, and I had just finished washing the dishes and tidying the kitchen.

Now it was my turn to relax. I was on my way to my bedroom, intent on writing a letter to Taddeo, when something compelled me to see if Charlotte was all right. It was unlike me. I still avoided her as much as possible, but the way she had looked during our meal—the flashes of pain on her face whenever she moved—shifted my hard, solid indifference ever so slightly.

"Alba," she said after I had knocked and entered the room. She was lying on her stomach, unmoving. "Sit down," she said, nodding towards the space beside her on the bed.

Why I sat is still a mystery to me. All I wanted to do was see if she needed anything. I didn't want to stay in that room with her lying on the same bed that she shared with my father. Perhaps I felt sorry for her. She looked helpless and small to me then. I sat down slowly so as not to shift the mattress beneath her already aching body. "How do you feel?" I asked.

"I'm okay, as long as I don't move."

She smiled. I did not.

"You are taking medicine?"

"Yes, but it doesn't always help. It just makes me sleepy."

There was something I could do, but I was hesitant to tell her. I was afraid she would think I was primitive, a backwards girl fumbling with home remedies in this country of modern medicine. "I can get you something?" I asked.

She moved then, a slight shifting, and her face twisted as she stifled a cry. In that moment, this woman was no longer the object of my contempt as much as my pity. She was helpless, the framework of her body working against her, and my pride seemed small in comparison. "There is a treatment we do in San Vittorio," I said. "If you will let me, we can try it."

"Oh, yes," she said, "Please."

"It may seem—how do you say—strange."

"I'll try anything, Alba."

"I will need cloth. Perhaps a clean handkerchief I

can cut up?"

"Go into the top drawer of your father's night table. He has some in there."

Charlotte could not know that I had already discovered where my father kept his handkerchiefs. I chose one that looked a little frayed, then went to my room and retrieved three quarters from my purse. I went to the kitchen to get the rest of what I needed, passing my father and his friends so engrossed in their card game that they didn't even notice me. I returned to Charlotte with three small drinking glasses, a box of matches, some string, and a pair of scissors.

She did not question me as I cut the handkerchief into small squares. I wrapped one square around each of the quarters, tying them off with the string to form three little triangular bundles, each with a tuft of cloth sticking up.

"You must take off your blouse," I said.

Charlotte moved slowly, grimacing and grunting, as I helped her remove her blouse and then lay back down on her stomach.

After unclasping her brassiere, I arranged the three bundles on her back. "Don't move," I said.

When I lit the match, she twisted her head to see what I was doing. To her credit, she did not question me. I wondered how she could trust me, knowing how I felt about her.

"This will feel strange," I said, lighting the first tuft of cloth. "Your skin will tighten, but don't be alarmed. It will help you to feel better."

I placed a glass over the flame, and Charlotte's skin rose with the bundle on top, swelling into the glass like liquid flesh. The technique was ancient: the pain in her back would be relieved through the proper application of fire and air.

"Alba, what are you doing back there?"

"Am I hurting you?"

"No, but—."

"Then you must remain still."

I lit the other bundles, one at a time, placing a glass over each. Charlotte lay quietly as I worked. Maybe she did trust me, or maybe she was just too afraid to move, but she allowed me to repeat this ritual several times over the surface of her back. Each time I removed a glass, her skin melted back into place until all that was left when I was finished was a pattern of red circles across her white skin.

I refastened her brassiere, then got her bathrobe from the closet and placed it over her back. "You should feel better soon," I said.

"I've never felt anything like that before. What were you doing?"

I explained it to her, and she listened with what seemed like true interest. The judgment I had feared never surfaced as I described the many ways we took care of ourselves in San Vittorio. I recounted to Charlotte how, whenever my brother was sick or injured, my mother allowed me to treat him under her supervision. When a cut on his foot had become infected, she watched me apply a sliced potato with baking soda to draw the infection out. When he complained of an earache, she guided me in suctioning off the fluid from his ear canal with a hollow tube made of linen and wax. I had watched her do this in the homes of afflicted neighbors. It began with a pencil, a candle, and a strip of cloth. She would wrap the cloth tightly around the pencil, then light the candle and allow the wax to drip onto it, steadily turning the pencil until the entire strip was coated with it. With the pencil removed, a waxed cloth straw remained. The first time I had instructed Taddeo to lie on his side, infected ear upwards, he looked nervous, but he remained still as I inserted one end of the straw into his ear. I then lit the other end, causing the infected liquid to siphon off into the tube.

Charlotte gave me her full attention. She was able to sit up in bed, the bathrobe wrapped around her bare shoulders. This was the longest I had ever spent alone with her.

"You should rest now," I said.

"Please don't go yet, Alba."

I stiffened. I had treated her, and the very act of treatment is intimate in its own way. Yet I hoped she did not think this interaction, or the conversation that followed it, had made us friends.

"I know you don't like me," she continued. "I know you don't approve of the life your father has made with me here. But, please, just listen to me for a moment."

When we are children we cover our ears to block out the sounds we don't wish to hear. This is what I wanted to do. Instead, I remained still and allowed her to speak. She had found a sliver of an opening into my heart, and I allowed her the opportunity to squeeze herself in if she could. It was out of curiosity, I told myself, when I knew it was really because I wanted to have something to grasp, some small explanation that would give me some comfort in this awkward household. Harboring anger is exhausting, and I was becoming very, very tired.

"Sometimes," she said, "if we're lucky, we come across a person who makes all the difference in the world to us, someone we feel safe with, and who understands and accepts everything about us. I hope someday you meet a man like that, Alba, and then you'll understand. You'll see that some people are just meant to be together."

I nodded, not wanting to speak because if I did, the stinging in my eyes might turn to tears. I looked across the room to where the window showed a patch of the East River in the distance. Did my father ever look at that water and think of the blue Ionian?

I coughed before finding my voice. "Did he ever speak about us?"

"Oh, yes, of course he did. He never stopped loving you and your brother, but he couldn't live two lives."

"So he chose this one."

"Your mother—"

"I know. He told me."

"Alba, I love your father. I truly do, and he loves me. I have nothing else to say in my defense."

What could I say to that? I was beaten, at least for that night. I was tired and sad and lonely, and all I wanted was for someone to tell me what to do with my life.

"I miss my family," I said. "I miss my home."

She reached for me, but I was not yet ready for her embrace. I got up to leave.

"One day you'll understand," she said.

She did not know that I already did.

Chapter Sixteen

It took awhile before I could admit to myself how much I missed William. Nearly three weeks had passed since I had spoken to him, and I began to wonder if I had made a mistake in pushing him away. I had so few friends here in New York. With William exiled and Peggy . . . well, I had not seen Peggy in months. I had tried a few times to find her at the hotel, but I always seemed to miss her in her comings and goings. She worked only a few blocks from The Fig and Chestnut, yet she seemed beyond my reach. I hardly knew anything about her. I knew only that she had a younger brother and a sweetheart. I didn't know where she lived or anything about her parents and where they came from. Yet her bubbly chatter and her way of looking at the world as if it were powerless to ever knock her down kept me always on the lookout for her in the streets and shops around the neighborhood. I wanted to do something nice for her, to buy her a little gift or treat her to lunch, but Peggy seemed to have disappeared.

One Friday afternoon, I decided to try again to find

her and went to the hotel during my lunch break from the bakery. Avoiding the front desk so I would not run into William (I was not ready to talk to him yet) I slinked along the edges of the lobby and up to one of the mezzanines. As I looked for a staff person to ask where I could find Peggy, I heard a joyful laugh that could only belong to her. She stood by the elevators with two other girls, both of them wearing the uniform of the hotel maids.

Peggy's eyes widened when she saw me, and she gestured for me to join them. After introducing us to one another, she pulled me into the elevator with them when the doors opened.

"Where are we going?" I asked.

"To one of the guest rooms," said the girl called Mabel.

"We shouldn't be doing this," said Jane, the other. "We could lose our jobs."

"We won't lose our jobs," said Peggy. "The worst that could happen is that we get reprimanded."

I wasn't sure I wanted to be part of whatever it was they were doing, but I was so caught up in my curiosity and my happiness at having found Peggy that I went along with it.

Leaving the elevator, we walked quickly down the corridor and stopped at one of the guest rooms. Jane pulled a key from her uniform pocket and opened the door. Inside, we all settled on the floor in front of a brown polished cabinet with an opaque window set into it. Jane turned a knob, and the window came to life.

"There she is!" said Mabel. "There's my mother!"

A man's voice poured out of the cabinet, while in the window that same man addressed a smiling woman in a grocery store. I was mesmerized. I had heard of television, but I had never seen it, and now, there in front of me, a scene happening in another place was playing out in miniature. I watched as women answered questions and ran about the store in some type of game to win money and other prizes. I had gotten used to radio, to the disembodied voices coming from the wooden box in my father's living room, but what I witnessed there in that hotel room, bodies animated in a little window cut into a cabinet, went beyond my wildest imaginings.

I don't think Peggy and the girls noticed my fascination. They were engrossed in the program, cheering on Mabel's mother in whispered shouts. When the show was over, Mabel turned the knob, and the figures disappeared. We got up from the floor and stood behind the door as Jane peeked out into the corridor. "All clear," she said, and we slipped out.

When the elevator doors opened in the lobby, the girls stopped their excited chatter, and Jane and Mabel went off to do their jobs as if nothing unusual had happened. To my relief, William was not at the front desk. Peggy gave me a quick hug and was about to dash away and out of my life again, but I wouldn't allow it this time. "Peggy," I said before she could vanish, "I'd like to meet you for lunch one day, if that is okay."

"That would be swell," she said. "I'll drop by the bakery this week." And in a flash, she was gone.

I don't know why Peggy's attention meant so much to me. Perhaps it was because I missed the company of females. There was Mrs. Santucci, but she was my boss, and Charlotte didn't count. So I left the hotel hungry but satisfied because I had spent my lunchtime experiencing something extraordinary, and on top of that, I had found Peggy again.

I was late getting back to The Fig and Chestnut. Mrs. Santucci came out from the back room wiping her hands on her apron as the bell on the door tinkled. She was about to say something when a customer came in, and I hurried to take his order.

The Santuccis were going to Philadelphia for the weekend to attend the wedding of Mr. Santucci's niece. They planned to leave that evening, entrusting me to close up The Fig and Chestnut all by myself. Mrs. Santucci's cousin, himself a baker, would open and oversee the shop on Saturday and Sunday while his son ran their family bakery in the Bronx.

In the late afternoon, Mrs. Santucci removed her apron and got ready to leave. "Are you sure you'll be okay?" she asked.

"Yes, I will be fine."

Several customers came into the shop after that, and I handled them confidently and without error. Three hours later, I was grateful that all had gone well when I came out from behind the counter and turned the sign on the door so that "closed" appeared on the outside.

There was a broom closet in the back room that held cleaning supplies and a mop. Mrs. Santucci always insisted on a clean floor for the next day, so I made that my first priority. I was about to haul the bucket out of the closet when I heard the bell, and I realized that I had turned the sign but had not locked the door.

"We're closed," I called as I walked to the front of the shop.

William stood by the counter. He did not even pretend to be in a good mood. "Alba," he said, "we need to talk."

I didn't move. I said nothing.

"You really hurt my feelings," he said. "You shut me out like I don't count for anything. I know it may not seem like it sometimes, but fellas have feelings, too, you know."

My throat tightened, and I swallowed to keep from coughing. It seemed all my saliva had dried up.

"If you're having problems, Alba, I'd like to help. I thought we were getting along just fine. What happened?"

I knew I was hurting him. I knew he was frustrated and losing patience, but I could think of nothing to say in my defense, so I said the only thing that came to mind. "Please . . . I have to mop the floor."

I don't think I will ever forget the look on his face. It hung somewhere between sorrow and disgust. He turned and hurried out, slamming the door behind him with an angry ringing of the little bell.

I braced myself against the counter and breathed deeply, an ache in my stomach forcing me to lean forward. At my feet, the black and white tiles of the floor began to vibrate, coming in and out of focus like an accusation. At that moment, I wanted to be back home in San Vittorio, in Luca's arms, feeling his shirt against my cheek, his fingers playing through my hair. I wished for the countless times we had walked the mountain in the early evenings when the breeze cooled our sun-parched faces, and the insects buzzed around us as the day slowly shifted into night. It was a palpable pain, the absence of him, and I wondered how I would ever have the strength to push away from that counter and resume my responsibility of closing The Fig and Chestnut for the Santuccis.

But push away I did, as duty won out over emotion, and I found my way back to the closet and the waiting mop and bucket. I was about to fill the bucket at the big stainless steel sink when the bell on the front door tinkled again. I froze. I could not confront William a second time. All I wanted was to finish my chores, to get out of there and back to my bedroom, where I could curl up and shut out the world of New York, of America, of the need to make impossible decisions. I refused to go to the front of the shop. William would have no choice but to go away, so I stood beside the open broom closet, not daring to move. I waited for the little bell to signal his departure, yet after what seemed like several minutes, still the bell had not chimed.

The sound of hard soles on the tile told me that William was walking to the back room. They were slow steps, deliberate in their casualness. Dread mingled with anticipation. Why did he come back? What would he say and do when he saw me?

The footsteps stopped outside the doorway, beyond my line of vision. I waited, but he did not enter. Finally, I couldn't stand it anymore. I walked to the doorway to confront him, but it was not William who stood there.

I felt a sudden rush of nausea as Vincenzo's mouth curled into a smile. He walked towards me, and I instinctively backed up, nearly stumbling over the bucket behind me.

"The door was open," he said in Italian, "but the sign says you're closed."

"We are closed. What do you want?"

"Such a hostile tone. I just want to buy some bread. You would not begrudge me some bread, would you?" He began to inch closer.

I gripped the handle of the mop. "You need to leave. Now!"

"No. I came here to buy bread."

"We have no more bread. Get out."

"Is this how you treat a customer?"

"I told you we're closed."

He took another step forward, and I pulled the mop in front of me, holding it out like a weapon. He laughed.

"You take pleasure in scaring women? You're a coward."

My face heated at the same time the rest of me went cold. I wanted to beat him with the mop, punch his face, push him against the ovens, and put an end to his vile behavior once and for all, but a chilling fear radiating through my body kept me rooted to the floor.

Suddenly, he was upon me. The mop clattered on the tiles as he pushed me against one of the baking racks, my back slamming into the metal shelving. Pinning his body against me, he clamped his hand over my mouth, and with his lips grazing my ear, in a whisper that repulsed and terrified me, he hissed his aversion of me: "I don't know who you think you are, princess, but let me remind you that you are nothing more than a dirty little peasant from the same part of the world I come from. So stop being such a stuck-up bitch and treating men like me as if we are some kind of flea-bitten rodent that you can beat out of your cellar with a broom."

I struggled to break free, but he held me without effort. I could not move my head. From the corner of my eye, I saw the details of his face distorted by his closeness: the pores of his skin, the lines of his lips, the stubble of his shaved cheek. I felt his free hand beneath my skirt, roughly grabbing my thigh, squeezing my bottom, his fingers like snakes yanking at my underwear.

Time stopped. My mind went blank, and my

hearing numbed. In the next instant, I was underwater, gliding through the warm Ionian Sea, a blue-green light reflecting from above. I was Io, the unfortunate maiden, transformed by circumstances beyond her control into the white and shining heifer. Io, the innocent, tormented and driven to wander the world in misery before being restored to her natural form. Caressed by the warm water, my arms moved in graceful arcs, my legs flowing like ribbons behind me. I lifted my head up into the sunshine, filled my lungs with the warm sea air, my hair trailing saltwater, my face spangled with sea drops. I swam to the shore and found myself in San Michele, on the beach where several boys kicked a ball around the sand, while nearby a cluster of girls lay about on towels, chatting or dozing in the afternoon heat. Taddeo was there, too, smiling. He called to me, and I walked, dripping wet, over to where he stood holding a cookie fresh from our mother's kitchen. He offered it to me, but before I could take it, Luca snatched it and ran off, laughing, daring me to get it from him. In mock anger, I ran after him, and when I caught him he fell onto the sand, pulling me down with him. We rolled on the beach laughing, the cookie held high in Luca's hand as I reached for it again and again. I was about to give up when suddenly the weight of his body lifted from me, and I was in the back room of The Fig and Chestnut with my back against the bakery rack. Vincenzo lay half unconscious on the floor with blood running from his nose, his face red and bruised. Above him stood a panting William, his shirt torn beneath his open coat, his hands bloody. He was saying something to me while staring at Vincenzo, repeating it over and over, but I couldn't understand. Then, slowly, as if through a fog, I began to hear his words: "Call the police,

Alba. Call the police. I need to keep an eye on him."

There was a telephone on the wall by the doorway leading to the front of the shop. I eased over to it, never shifting my gaze from the two of them. I don't know how I managed to make that call, or what I said when I did, but soon two police cars screeched into the street, sirens wailing, and The Fig and Chestnut, my happy place of work, became a crime scene.

Uniformed officers barged in as a crowd formed outside. Before I knew what was happening, two of the policemen seized William while a third grappled to lift Vincenzo to his feet.

"Hey, no, wait!" William shouted as he struggled to break free.

"Stop!" I shouted even louder. "Leave him alone."

The two policemen loosened their grip on William but did not let him go.

"The one on the floor," I screamed. "Not him."

I rushed to William's side and tried to forcibly remove their hands from him. They yielded, and I crushed myself against William's coat, hanging on to him as if my life depended on it.

I'm not sure what happened after that. My head swirled. My mouth answered questions that later I could not recall. I remember sitting on a chair by Mr. Santucci's work table, watching an exhausted William talk to the police. One of the policemen brought me a glass of water. I held it cupped in my hands and waited for them to leave. As I stared, distanced from the scene as if I were watching a play, something in my brain forced me to check on what I most feared. Without looking down, I took stock of my body. There was no stickiness between my legs, no blood. I felt no pain, no physical injury of forced entry. I was unmolested.

Chapter Seventeen

I awoke the next morning to an aching back and hazy memories of the night before. I remembered that the police had driven William and me to the hospital, where we spent endless hours waiting in the emergency room. William called my father, who arrived with Charlotte shortly afterwards, the two of them white-faced and agitated. My father embraced me as he launched into a thousand questions, then released me into a plastic chair and sat beside me, clutching my hand. I rested my head on his shoulder and listened with closed eyes as William explained what had happened. I knew there would be police reports, the pressing of charges, a possible trial, but all I wanted was to go home and sleep. Finally, after being fully checked by a doctor and pronounced unharmed, I said goodbye to William, then waited with Charlotte on the sidewalk in front of the hospital while my father hailed a taxi to bring us home.

Now, opening my eyes to a new day, I found my father seated across the room in my desk chair, staring at me. He looked haunted, as if he had been kept awake all night by the sound of invisible dangers lurking in the walls. There were no good-morning pleasantries, no inquiries as to whether or not I had slept well. "I should have let you go home," he said. "I should have given you the money."

I had never told him about my earlier encounters with Vincenzo. Those were experiences I wanted to forget. And if I had told him, he would have tried to keep a tighter hold on me, would have insisted I go to the police, or worse, attempted to track down Vincenzo himself and confront him directly. For my father's safety, as well as my own freedom, I kept these incidents to myself. Now I wondered whether or not I had done the right thing.

"This was not your fault, papa."

He just sat there, staring and breathing heavily.

"This man," I said, "this person who did this, it was not the first time I had dealings with him."

My father's face collapsed. When he opened his mouth to speak, I jumped ahead and told my story, talking above him every time he interrupted. He got up from his chair and began pacing the room while I told him about all my clashes with Vincenzo, from the ship to the streets. I explained how I thought I could handle the situation on my own, how I didn't want to worry him, until finally he exploded.

"I am your father," he shouted. "I have a right to know."

I eased out of bed and went to him. Placing my arms around his neck, I kissed him on the cheek. "I'm sorry, papa. Forgive me."

"I'm your father," he said, pulling me closer. "I'm supposed to protect you."

I gently pulled away. "I have to call the bakery," I said. "I have to explain to Mrs. Santucci's cousin what happened."

"Alba, a crime was committed there. I'm sure the police already spoke to him. But make your call anyway. Tell Mrs. Santucci's cousin to tell Mrs. Santucci that you will not be going back there to work."

My stomach dropped. I shook my head hard. "No, papa." I was not about to lose my job over this, not because of what happened to me there, not because of Vincenzo, not because of anything. The Fig and Chestnut was part of my everyday world, my life of stability in the chaos of my thoughts. I needed this job, not just for the money I earned or for the freedom it gave me to go out into the city and look after myself. I needed it because it offered me an anchor in my own stormy sea.

I followed my father as he blustered to the telephone in the hallway. Charlotte had come out of the kitchen and watched us from a distance, a dish towel and wet glass in her hand. I grabbed at my father's arm as he dialed information and asked to be connected to The Fig and Chestnut, but he held me off. I heard him speak to the person at the bakery, explain who he was, accept commiserations for what had happened to his daughter, then offer his apologies that this daughter could no longer continue her job.

There were tears in my eyes as he dropped the receiver into its cradle, and I pulled at him in a rage when he tried to walk away.

"Haven't I been through enough?" I shouted at his retreating back. A moment later, I heard his bedroom door close.

Charlotte placed the towel and glass on the dining room table and came towards me, but I ran to my room. With tears pouring down my face, I got dressed, grabbed my purse, and left the apartment. I hurried to Lexington Avenue, then ran south as street after street dissolved in a whirl behind me, my chest heaving and my lungs aching. When I could no longer breathe, I slowed to a walk all the way to the hotel. I wanted to see William. I knew I was out of control and needed his calm stability and common sense.

He was on the telephone when I walked up to the reception desk. Looking surprised, he motioned for me to wait, so I sat on one of the sofas in the lobby. A few minutes later he was sitting beside me. "How are you feeling?" he asked.

"I am okay," I said. It was only a partial lie; physically, except for a sore back, I was fine.

"You're here alone?"

"Yes."

"You should be home resting. You've been through a lot. I was going to come over after my shift to check on you, make sure you were all right."

"I wanted to properly thank you, William."

He looked down at the carpet and shook his head. "You don't have to thank me. I did what any man would have done in that situation. Thank God I came back when I did, though."

"Yes, thank God. But why did you come back? I had been so rude to you."

He took a deep breath and looked at the ceiling, then sat back against the sofa and crossed his arms. He turned his face to me. "I wasn't about to give up, Alba. I was angry, and I wanted answers."

I knew he was right. I knew he deserved answers, but how could I express how difficult it had been for me to give them? Sometimes, it felt as if there were walls separating me from myself, the true Alba, the Alba who loved and grieved and longed for happiness.

I couldn't give him an explanation for why that Alba could never tell him how much she appreciated his warmth, his humor, his patience with her unkindness. That Alba had been unable to tell him how much she adored the color of his eyes and the deep resonance of his laughter, how much she wanted to spend more time with him and meet his family and invite him over for Sunday dinners again and again and again.

But what had happened the night before shook my foundation, fracturing the plaster that held the true Alba prisoner. I could peek out now, even reach an arm out into the open. I hoped that in time the newly formed fissure would split apart for good and release me.

I told him about Vincenzo. It was the second time that morning I had told the story of my encounters, and when I had finished, William asked the same question my father had asked earlier that morning: why had I not told him this before?

I shrugged. A few moments passed while he waited for an answer. I shrugged again, and he put his arm around me. If he had pressed me, I would have gotten up and left, crushed, feeling there was not a soul in the world I could turn to for comfort.

"I have to get back to work," he said. "I'll call you later, before I come over, but right now I'm going to call your father." He silenced my protest by placing two fingers on my lips. "You should not be wandering around the city by yourself. I'm going to call your father to come and take you home."

He kissed me on the cheek and left, and I sat back into the comfort of the sofa. In the aftermath of my flight from the apartment that morning, my anger towards my father had lessened, and now, calmer, I really did not want to be alone. I felt exposed and vulnerable, even as I sat in the lobby of a fine hotel with hundreds of people milling about and no chance of my attacker appearing because he was safely locked away. It was odd to sense a presence of danger knowing there was none. Still, the fear was real and clung to me like a dark garment as I waited.

The day was bright with sunshine, although the early spring air was chilly. My father bought us an early lunch of egg salad sandwiches and coffee, and we walked over to Bryant Park so that we could eat them under the newly budding trees. We settled onto a bench, and my father handed me my food.

"Bettina Santucci called," he said, "soon after you left this morning. She wanted to know if you were all right."

"And what did you tell her?"

"I told her that physically you were fine, but that you had suffered a trauma and would not be coming back to work for a few days, or longer if needed. She agreed."

My coffee cup halfway to my mouth, I stopped and looked at him.

"Perhaps I was wrong," he said.

My eyes burned with an upwelling of affection for him. I tried to hide it by looking away, scanning the park with feigned interest. Across the giant lawn, the public library sat like a solid testament to the world's accumulated knowledge. How many millions of books did such a grand building hold? I thought of my own small collection stacked on my desk in my bedroom, how I had carried those books so lovingly across the sea, and how Vincenzo had abused them so maliciously.

My father nodded towards the library. "Have you

seen the inside?"

"No."

"It looks like a palace, with marble walls and lots of rooms. There are paintings everywhere, on the walls and the ceilings, and a huge room filled with long tables where anyone can go and read. Would you like to go and see it?"

"Papa," I said, "stop being kind to me."

He lowered his half-eaten sandwich. "What a strange thing to say."

"This morning, when you called the bakery, I wanted to hurt you. Physically hurt you."

"I know."

I stared at the paved walkway at my feet. Above my head, birds twittered. A squirrel scurried across the grass beneath one of the trees. It froze, then ran off in the opposite direction.

"Alba, I don't always know how to be a good father to you. I do what I think is best. I want you to have a good life, to have opportunities that you can't get in San Vittorio. But maybe I've been wrong about that, too. If you are so unhappy that all you want to do is work to get away from here, then I will buy the ticket for you."

He waited for my reaction, but none came. I stared at him blankly as a tidal wave of images flashed across my mind: William holding my hand as we walked down Broadway in the snow-laden night; mopping the face of a woman in labor as my mother delivered a breach in a low-lit bedroom; standing on the street beside my father looking into the bright, wide lobby of a hospital; walking with Taddeo down the mountain to San Michele to buy coffee at the outdoor market; exploring the canyons of Manhattan wearing new shoes, new clothes, with new ideas in my head; the sweet fresh air of Calabria; the lights of Times Square. All moved rapidly in a dizzying kaleidoscope of times and places in my imagination.

Suddenly, I went blank, the carnival of colors and sounds abruptly shut off.

"Thank you," I said.

We rode the uptown bus back to the apartment. My father spoke now and then about mundane things, and I responded mechanically, trying not to show my lack of interest. I was tired and emotionally drained. Only once did I react sincerely, when he said he would send my mother a telegram that evening telling her what had happened. I didn't want her or Taddeo to find out because there was nothing either of them could do from across the ocean except worry. We argued, but I won in the end. I could tell he didn't want to upset me.

When we got home, there was a letter from my mother waiting for me. Since arriving in New York, I had never corresponded with her. Taddeo served as our envoy, and later, when I became angry at her for what I thought of as her deceit, I never even asked about her in my letters to my brother. He faithfully told me anyway. She was well, he said, always well, and so I was surprised to come home that day and find her letter on my bed where Charlotte had put it after the morning's mail had arrived.

"Papa," I said, holding the envelope as I approached him in the hallway. "Did something happen back home?" I was afraid to open the letter.

He took it from me, examined the envelope, and handed it back. "The postal service is slow in San Vittorio," he said. "Or else she took a long time to answer. I wrote to her some time ago."

He turned towards the living room, to listen to one

of his radio programs, no doubt, but he could not just leave me like that without an explanation. "What is going on, papa? Why did you write to my mother?"

"Because I needed her help," he said.

He left me standing there with the envelope in my hand, too worried to open it, too curious not to.

Back in my room, I sat on my bed and placed the envelope on the bedspread, staring at my name and my father's address in my mother's spidery handwriting. My anger towards her had since disintegrated. All I felt now was a longing to be with her again, a yearning for her strength and kindness. I could not know as I picked up the envelope and tore it open that its contents would influence the rest of my life.

I unfolded the paper and read:

My dearest Alba,

I hope you are well and know how much I miss you. Taddeo has kept me informed about all that happens in New York, but I had hoped you would write to me yourself, at least a letter or two. I suspect you're upset with me for sending you to your father without telling you everything, but you're old enough to know that life is no simple matter and that marriage is not always what it seems. I hope in time you'll realize that what I did, I did for your own good. You were reluctant to leave, and I don't blame you for that, but if I had told you what to expect when you arrived in America, you would have refused to go. I know you respect my wishes, but you've always been a headstrong girl, and even you have limits on what you will do for your mother.

I want only joy for you, Alba, and there has been

no joy since your Luca died. I watched you wither from that day forward. Truly, I cannot imagine what it's like to lose your childhood love. When he was taken from you so brutally, I grieved with you because I could see that he had taken a part of you with him to the grave, and I wondered if you would ever be able to let him go. I know you loved him deeply, but you needed to find a life without him. I hope and pray that you find that kind of love again in America, where new opportunities are waiting for you.

Do not be angry with your father. Some things are just not meant to be. When he first told me he had found another woman, it saddened me, but I soon realized that you cannot own another person. He found the kind of love that I couldn't give him, so why should I wish him bitterness? Your father has always taken care of us. He still does, so do not blame him.

And do not hate Charlotte. She gave your father a life of happiness in a place he had come to feel was his home. He would not love her if she were a bad person. As long as she treats you well, you should respect her and be appreciative that she has welcomed you. Anger and animosity will only make you sick.

I hope and pray you will forgive me for any pain I may have caused you.

With great affection,
Mama

I released the letter. It fluttered onto the bedspread, a giant clumsy butterfly, where it remained as I lay down beside it and wept.

Chapter Eighteen

That spring of 1948 slowly eased into summer. I discovered that heat in New York was held captive by towering buildings and concrete, worsened by the exhaust of buses and cars. Yet instead of hindering the glitzy passage of life on the streets, the summer's heat fueled it so that fire escapes became balconies, restaurants and cafés moved tables out onto the pavement, and the sounds of chatter and laughter in the pepper-hot air echoed well into the deepest hours of the night.

One Sunday, William and I took refuge in the salty breezes of Rockaway. To my surprise and delight, Peggy had invited us to join her and her sweetheart Bobby for a day out at the beach. Bobby had a car, she said, and would pick us up. We waited for them on the street in front of my father's building, William in a tee shirt and shorts, and I in a beach robe covering my bathing suit. I had packed some snacks, two towels, and suntan lotion—an apparent necessity for American skin—in a big canvas bag. When a bare-chested Bobby stopped his car in front of the building,

Peggy, in sunglasses and a gauzy white shift over a pink bathing suit, waved out the window of the passenger seat, a half-peeled orange in her hand. "Get in," she called.

William and I climbed into the back seat. "I would have preferred Coney Island," he whispered to me after Bobby had turned the car onto First Avenue.

"I heard that," said Peggy. She threw a slice of orange at William, who caught it and threw it back.

"Hey, quit horsing around," said Bobby.

I did not know what horses had to do with anything, but by now I had gotten used to figuring out American expressions I didn't understand.

Peggy gently slapped his arm and he chuckled. He was a big-boned blond with an oversized grin, and he matched Peggy perfectly in energy and enthusiasm.

The hot summer breeze washed in through the rolled down windows as we left Manhattan over the Queensborough Bridge. It was a long ride to Rockaway, passing through neighborhoods of neat houses and well-kept yards, with children playing on grass instead of in streets. William looked out his window with a wistful smile as if he were remembering something from long ago or dreaming of something to come.

"What are you thinking?" I asked.

"You see these homes?" he said. "One day I'm going to own one just like them. And, hopefully, have a wife and some kids to share it with." He narrowed his eyes and smiled broadly at me, then winked. "What do you think?"

"I think it sounds wonderful," I said.

He took my hand and squeezed it, and I rode the rest of the way with my head on his shoulder, watching the landscape of William's dream roll by in the streets outside.

Rockaway had an amusement park, a sprawling village of mechanical rides set within the streets across from the beach. Inside, hordes of merrymakers screamed joyfully while being twirled and hurtled through the air.

"Playland," said Peggy as we walked beneath a sign of a giant clown's face and two detached hands pointing the way to fun and adventure. A hump-backed skeleton of a roller coaster towered high above the park's walls and rattled with every twist and turn of its plunging cars. "We can come here later tonight, after the sun goes down. We'll have a gas."

When we reached the boardwalk, Peggy and Bobby headed straight for the beach. It swarmed with people, some stretched out on blankets or lounge-like folding chairs to soak in the sun, others shaded beneath colorful umbrellas. Out in the ocean, bodies bobbed and splashed, watched over by lifeguards in their high wooden chairs. Occasionally, a warning whistle called someone back who had swum too far, and everywhere the sounds of laughter, shouts, and chatter were carried on the hot, salty air.

"Come on," said Peggy. "I see a spot over by the rocks."

She pulled Bobby along towards the stairs that led to the beach below, but I held William back. He looked at me quizzically. "I'd like to walk with you a little," I said.

"Sure." He called after Peggy and Bobby. "Go on ahead, you two. We'll be down soon."

Peggy waved a hand above her head without turning back, and we watched them sprint to the water towards a tiny patch of unclaimed sand beside a boulder jetty.

We strolled hand in hand to the cawing of gulls and the strong, steady shush of breaking waves. When we stopped at the railing to look at the horizon, William put his arm around my shoulder and held me close. A lone ship floated somewhere in the distance, bound for God knows where. I leaned into William as I scanned the beach spread out before us like a living painting: a small boy dumping sand from a toy pail onto the head of a smaller boy, who immediately began to wail; a woman with a big straw hat sitting on a beach chair reading a book; shouts of "ice-cream, cold drinks" permeating the air from a man in swimming trunks with a large white case strapped in front of him trudging among the beachgoers.

It was all so comforting, so extraordinary in its simplicity, that a warmth enveloped me from the inside out, and I felt a surge of gratitude. My life had begun to take shape. With my father's help, I had enrolled in nursing school and would start as soon as the summer was over. And while I still missed my family back home, there was hope in our future that we would not have to suffer our separation forever. Taddeo had written telling me our father had agreed to sponsor him to come to America in two and a half years, when he turned eighteen. He, too, would go to school here. He would study and become a famous architect, he said, like the people who designed the Empire State Building. Then it would just be a matter of time before our mother joined us.

"William," I said, remembering something, "did I ever tell you about the time my mother and I delivered a baby for a woman who had too many relatives?"

He crinkled his face in the way I had come to love, the way that told me I amused and delighted him.

"No, Alba, you most certainly did not."

"Well, this woman had so many relatives that when they came to visit her in bed after the baby was born, they filled the room so much that the floor collapsed."

"No!" he said. "You're making this up!"

"I am not. Fortunately, the baby was safe in another room, and no one was killed. But some were hurt, including the baby's mother. People talked about it for weeks afterwards."

William looked skeptical. "Did that really happen?"

"Yes, it did."

"What made you think of it now?"

"I'm not sure. Maybe it's because there are so many people out there." I swept my arm across the railing. "So many, many people."

William shook his head and chuckled. "That's a crazy story."

I snuggled against him and deeply inhaled the fresh air. "William, I want you to meet my mother someday."

"I'd like that, Alba."

I closed my eyes, wishing my mother were already there to meet William. It was her letter that had been my tipping point, her revelation about Luca that had struck me so hard I could no longer deny the blood she had drawn.

Luca's death had been unexpected, swift as a flood and just as devastating. It happened in 1943, on one of those clear, blazing summer days when the Mediterranean sun scorches the faces of laborers in the fields and old people sit outside doorways fanning themselves with handkerchiefs. Luca and I had walked with a group of friends down the mountain to San Michele to have a picnic lunch on the beach. We were seven teenagers, a mixed bunch of clowning boys and laughing girls, strong-limbed and loud. We ambled off the mountain and crossed into town, past the houses and businesses that lined the main road, and onto the stretch of pebbly, sandy shore that curved uninterrupted along the coast of the Ionian Sea.

We found a place on the beach to lay our blankets, and the boys put down the bags they had been carrying that held our food. We girls unpacked the lunch and handed out the sandwiches of tomato and mozzarella on crusty home-baked bread. We doled out portions of green salad into small bowls we had taken with us and washed it all down with bottles of mineral water.

"I wish we had brought some wine," said Marta.

"Wine would make us sleepy in this heat," I said.

"Then we could nap," said Alberto. "What better place to sleep than on a beach, with the fresh sea air and the music of the waves?"

Maria chimed in. "My mother said we can't have wine if we go swimming. People have died that way."

"Well," said Marco, "I'm going for a swim right now." He grabbed Serena's hand and pulled her up from the blanket. "Let's go."

Serena got up and the two of them trotted off. A few moments later, we heard them laughing and yelping as they splashed in the water.

Luca asked if I wanted to join them, but I remained on the sand as I watched him walk off to the sea.

The day passed lazily. While my friends swam, sunbathed, and walked along the shore, I dozed on the blanket or read my copy of Bontempelli's *The Boy with Two Mothers*. Later in the afternoon, I took a break from the heat and walked down to the water to cool my feet. Only Luca and Alberto were swimming now. Alberto floated serenely on his back, close to shore, but Luca was farther out, bobbing and gliding on the horizon. He noticed me, even from a distance, and waved both arms in the air. I watched him dive beneath the waves, knowing how much he enjoyed the energy of the sea, while I let the water rolling up to shore cover my ankles, recede, and come back again. It was hypnotic, this repeated surging and withdrawing in a rhythm as old as the earth, giving the illusion that it was I who was moving rather than the water.

A dripping Alberto came trudging onto shore. "Is there any food left? I'm hungry."

"There might be," I said. "I think Maria packed up what was left."

He squeezed my arm as he passed. "Thanks."

"Wait," I called. "I'll come with you. I'm a little hungry, too."

Back at the blankets, we found Marta and Maria stretched out with closed eyes, exposing their already bronzed limbs to the full force of the sun, and Marco and Serena playing a game of cards. "Who brought those?' I asked.

"Marco is never without a deck of cards," said Serena.

"Want to play?" asked Marco.

"I want to eat," said Alberto, on his knees and searching through one of the bags.

"See if there's any salad left," I said, sitting down beside Serena to watch the game. "I'd like a little if it's not all gone."

Silverware clinked against bowls as Alberto moved the contents of the bag. "Sorry, no salad," he said. "But there are two sandwiches. Do you want one?"

I held out my hand to take the sandwich from him

when suddenly he froze.

"What's wrong?" I asked.

"Be quiet!" Alberto jumped to his feet. His face had gone white.

We all heard it then, the familiar humming, the death music that clamped our throats into momentary paralysis. For one panicked instant, none of us could move. And then they appeared, metal dragons cutting the azure sky and spitting fire. Immediately, we jumped up from the blankets to the sound of terrified screams as everyone on the beach scattered and fled.

"Get to the road," Alberto shouted. There was shelter there, if we made it, behind buildings and cars, but as my friends scrambled across the sand towards safety, I turned towards the water, towards Luca. I tried to see him in the sea amid swimmers racing towards the beach. Alberto's arm around my waist yanked at me. I struggled and kicked, but Alberto dragged me away, cursing the planes and shouting that there was nothing I could do. Tears blurring my vision, I stumbled beside him, fighting him, until finally his strength won out and I gave in.

Water and sand spouted up in choreographed lines as the bullets rained down. Bodies pitched forward into the sand, and in the distance, lifeless swimmers bobbed in a sea tinged with red.

It was over in a matter of minutes. The noise of rapid fire ceased as abruptly as it had begun, the blaring whirr of propellers lessened as the planes withdrew, and our ears were left ringing in a pure and terrible silence.

We crouched under the bright blue sky behind a wall in someone's front yard. Marta's leg was bleeding. Maria was shaking. Serena clung to Marco, who sat with his back to the wall and stared straight ahead. Alberto slowly got up, his jaw clenched and twitching, when he saw that I was about to go back to the beach.

"I'll go with you," he said. He took my hand, and together we walked across the road towards the gathering crowd. I did not hurry. I did not want to see what my heart already knew.

When we got close enough, Alberto tried to shield me from the sight of Luca's body, but I pushed him away and continued on. Luca had made it to the shore. He lay face down, halfway in the water, the other half on the wet, pebbly sand, with bullet holes in his back. I knelt beside him and brushed aside the hair that was plastered to his cheek. Alberto, in a strained voice, tried to rouse me, but I could not move, could not breathe, until the tears overcame me like a hot, raging flood. I threw myself across Luca's shoulders and sobbed violently against his dripping skin until the authorities came and pried me from his body.

"Would you like to go down to the water now?" William asked. His blue eyes seemed to shimmer in the sunlight.

"Sure," I said.

"Did I mention how nice you look in that—what do you call it—that thing you girls wear over your bathing suits?"

I flushed. I was still not good at accepting compliments from him, even though we were now "going steady" as they said in America.

We found a ramp that led down to the beach. "Give me your shoes," I said when we reached the sand. We removed our sandals, and I put them in the canvas bag William had been carrying for me.

"Don't step on any shells," he said. "You don't

want to cut yourself."

"Don't worry. Saltwater heals."

We found Peggy and Bobby stretched out on a blanket where they had first claimed their spot, the sun glinting off their sunglasses, and walked past them to the water's edge. Standing side by side, with hands clasped and looking out to sea, we let the water cover our ankles, then felt our feet sink into the sand as the water pulled out again in sparkling ribbons, never tiring of the sensation that we were moving.

About the Author

Lisa Sita is a native and resident of Queens, New York, where she writes in various genres and teaches anthropology. Her professional background includes work as a museum educator, curriculum writer, student advisor, and author of non-fiction books for young readers. Lisa holds a Master of Fine Arts in Writing and a Bachelor of Arts and Master of Arts in Anthropology. Visit her website at lisasita.com.